HARVEST OF ATHENAS

Michael Andre-Driussi

Sirius Fiction

ISBN-13: 978-1-947614-17-8 (paperback)
ISBN-13: 978-1-947614-18-5 (ebook)

CONTENTS

Title Page

Copyright

Freaks Like Us, Born to Rule   1

Psi Prison   9

Digger's Daughter, Tiny   31

Speculative Envoy   52

Vitamin Double-D   57

Your Life Is Mine   83

The Donkey's Tale   101

Stories to the Future   108

Master Wu of Bamiyan   128

Ghost Heart of San Francisco   145

Paradise Axis   180

Publishing History   217

Books By This Author   219

FREAKS LIKE US, BORN TO RULE

Some are born freaks,
some achieve freakdom,
and some have freakdom thrust upon them.

President Elephant Man began his unprecedented fourth term, a historic moment for the ages.

It was a time when American freakocracy seemed as wheezing as a claptrap calliope, an era when the government employed fifty-nine percent of the population, from the one percenters, those natural freaks of little people, pinheads, giants, albinos, conjoined twins, and others; through the skeletal bonies, at two percent; the morbidly obese "mo'bese" at seven percent; and the tattooed inkies at fourteen percent; down to the "nearly common" obese at thirty-five percent.

Against this backdrop, boy met girl at a place where sand met sea. It was an Atlantic pleasure town whose weathered highway sign showed frolicking lobster-boys, their digits fused into fleshy claws, and svelte seal-girls whose fingers came out of their shoulders. It was a location where the humid night air carried trace aromas of sun-softened road tar and candy apple.

He was Bullock, a thirty-seven-year old eunuch from inland.

She was Wispy the Bearded Lady, a twenty-three-year old local at the shore.

She had stormy eyes that flashed at the sound of lies, but those same gray peepers were dazzled by the headlights of a customized Bricklin SV-5, then by the first sight of its driver Bullock, who seemed a lifting rocket come to stir new life in the feeble freaks. Against her will she felt her heart rev up in tandem along with Bullock's racecar.

And Bullock saw something in her, something he could not name. Yes, she was a local princess, albeit of a place that was fading fast. But there was something more than this, a kinship, a soul-yearning recognition.

"I wanna be your fren," he said. "I wanna gird yer dreams an' secrets."

"Hmm."

"Togever we could break dis trap. We'll run till we drop, we'll never go back."

"Oo."

"Someday we're gonna get to that palace an' we'll swim in the pool."

"Ah!"

"'Cause freaks like us, baby, we was born to rule."

So she got into his high status car and they blasted off, true to his word.

After an intimacy or three she came to understand he was a gaff. Previously he had been Bulky the obese, who failed at becoming morbidly obese, and before that Bonewell the skeleton.

For his part, he was pretty sure she was a gaff. Formerly known as Windy the Bonemaiden. She claimed that the anorexia kept her hormones down, suppressing her natural freak from expressing.

It was a time when the government was sinking under its own stupendous weight, when the cheap talk of "reform" had given way to Gaff Prison, the penitentiary for pretenders, jail for the gyppers.

As always, the rules were rather vague. The natural freaks were in the clear. Tension arose in the border between freaks natural and those self-made: bonies seemed fairly safe, as did the mo'bese and the obese; the inkies were safe so long as their expensive tattoos were real.

Bullock and Wispy held each other in love and ambition, but also as cross-hostages. Both were fake one-percenters, ersatz elites.

The night highway rolled on endlessly. The

sticky feel of warm leatherette. That certain ache in the lower back from spending too many hours in the car. At the point when your mouth feels as fuzzy as the dice hanging from the rearview mirror, then it is time to stop for a long rest.

Bullock's career rocket continued to rise as they visited town after town. First he was a beadle (E2) at the Ministry of Athletics, marshaled by a mo'bese dean (O4); then he transferred to be a verger (E3) at the Ministry of Basketball, led by a little person archdeacon (02). It did not seem to matter what snake oil he was selling, the freaks ate it up. The piles of cash the couple was making enabled both to keep a steady stream flowing back to their families.

❊ ❊ ❊

Then one day she said, "Bullock, baby, I'm pregnant."

It gave him pause.

She watched him carefully.

His face lit up with a brilliant smile.

"I think you should meet my folks," he said. "Stay with them a while."

She liked that idea.

"I think we should get married," he said. "A secret marriage."

She didn't like that idea.

But her uncle Fullton did, very much, and he was the head of her family.

Wispy had a good time living in the countryside. Bullock told people she was away on sabbatical, and in fact she studied a great deal as she grew heavy with child.

Bullock's rise passed through a kaleidoscope of stations, including a season as an almoner (E4) at the Ministry of Melanin, under the auspices of an albino diocesan (O7); a quickie as an anagnost (E7) at the Ministry of Solitude, captained by a conjoined twin suffragan (O6); to at last a canon (O1) at the Ministry of Rocket Science, presided over by a pinhead prelate (O8).

The baby was born, a heartbreakingly healthy boy she named "Satellite of Love," and assigned others adroitly adopted him.

Then Wispy went back to Bullock where she submitted to the secret marriage.

❃ ❃ ❃

That should have been the happy ending. That seemed to be the moment from which it would all be smooth rocketing up through the levels of society: through The Privileged to The Powerbrokers, The Big Wigs, perhaps even The Head Honchos.

But something went wrong.

On the national scale, the sainted President Elephant Man had died, initiating the moral panic that would later be dubbed the Year of Three Presidents.

At the personal scale, someone on Bullock's side sniggered like his guy had gotten away with something. Uncle Fullton panicked, sensing a threat to his family's income stream, and he publicly disclosed the marriage between Bullock and Wispy. This triggered a social storm, so Bullock sent Wispy to a safehouse.

Unfortunately, this escalated the crisis. Fullton hired a group of men who ambushed Bullock at a highway rest area. Three held him down and the specialist castrated him, making the gaff into a genuine.

The scent of fresh blood overpowering the mothballs in the urinals, Bullock stood up alone in the restroom. Hunched over and weak, he staggered out to the parking lot, only to find that his assailants had absconded with his beloved car. His legs buckled, and he dropped down to his knees where the pain in his torn groin made him cry out in agony.

At that moment a car on the highway turned in and its headlights blinded Bullock. The vehicle, an open top sports car, raced over to stop beside him.

"Hey, Bullock!" cried the familiar voice of an old buddy. "You okay? Need a ride?"

Thus began his recovery.

It had been three years since he met Wispy. Now forty years old, Bullock dedicated himself to the Mansion of the Unmanned. But paradoxically he was possessed by a jealousy toward Wispy, believing her to have betrayed him with at least three lovers.

But Wispy was "Wavy" now, her new beard heavy and thick.

Bullock urged her to dedicate herself to the Mansion of the Hermaphrodite.

She resisted, saying, "I got no interest in being a Paragon."

"Ya got a lover, then?"

"Of course not! I's never into sexual congress, as you know full well. You pressured me into it. Ya got nobody to blame but youself."

"That being the case, why not become a Paragon? Seems natural for ya."

"Maybe 'cuz I's sick of you tellin' me what to do!"

❊ ❊ ❊

In the end, though, she did become Paragon of Hermaphrodites, as he became Paragon of Unmanned, each in their mansion of glory, forever separate, forever equal.

Their son, Satellite of Love, never could attain freakdom, even with all the nepotism and string-pulling his biological parents could provide across the many years. They were eager to help, and he had so many options: he could purge himself into a bonie, he could bulk into a mo'bese, or at the very least he could ink up, but he refused all, or simply failed. Was it due to an over-identification with his foster parents, or was it a scathing rejection of his birth parents? Who can guess the spite of one's children? Perhaps he even worked at a Gaff Prison, that exclusive employer for those of his ilk. In any event, he died in his late twenties as a mere mark, a chump, a lugen.

A few years after that, Bullock got the last word. On his deathbed, he dictated this message to Wavy: "Fakes like us, baby, we was born to rule!"

PSI PRISON

In the psionic wing of a prison located somewhere in the Evolutionary Republic of America, the cell door slammed behind Cyan.

He stood there for a moment, observing the room. As prison cells go, the place was not bad, but he had no illusions: he expected to stay there in solitary confinement until he was hauled out and shot. It was a surprising fate for a decorated Hero of the Evolution.

Paradoxically, what he felt was relief. All the months of tension were now gone. The raid at three a.m. meant there was still an hour or two before the winter dawn, so he lay down and dropped into happy sleep just after the light went out.

When the light came on again, he saw the color photo of Blue Steel, supreme leader of the Evolution, hanging over his bed on the wall, just as on the walls of the other cells, and on the walls of the houses, the towns, throughout the nation.

The first day in prison is like the first day in school. Cyan knocked on his cell door the first five beats of "Shave and a Haircut" to announce his presence.

In reply the door finished the phrase with a "tap-tap," even though he could see through the spy hole there was nobody standing there.

By this Cyan knew there was a telekinetic nearby, in the cell opposite or one of its neighbors.

He whispered, "Can you hear me?"

There was no response.

He held up three fingers.

Three taps sounded on the door.

So the TK was also a clairvoyant Esper. Cyan tried a sentence in sign language.

There was no response.

Cyan went to the window overlooking the prison yard covered with snow. He breathed upon the glass, and with his finger wrote, "Who?"

On the window, ghostwriting formed: "303."

So it was the cell straight across.

Cyan fogged the glass and wrote, "Name?"

Below this, TK force wrote: "Name?"

Cyan scoffed at this time-wasting, but then he shrugged. He traced his name on the glass.

There was a pause, then appeared the word: "Impossible!"

"Give me telepaths," wrote Cyan.

"Give me woman."

"How?"

"Recent nude."

Cyan mulled it over and eventually sent a fifteen second image of his last lover taking off her dress.

* * *

Cyan received a telepathic burst:

Greetings, Cyan. This is 310. Your cell was emptied about a week ago, but I do not think it ever had an inhabitant more illustrious than yourself. You know the type of exchange system we have here, and I hope you possess a fairly refined palette since I am a gourmand, trading in food memories rather than smutty clips of naked ladies.

He went on to describe in high detail the sort of gustatory sensations he most desired. Then he sketched out the telepath network among the prisoners: who had what, and what each desired for trade.

* * *

The teleporters were all dead except for one, Blue Wind himself. The rarest of the psionic adepts, the jaunters had been ghostly thieves and assassins for the Evolution until the first turning when they were hunted down and executed. That was when Blue Wind was declared anti-evolutionary.

Cyan recalled a time as a teen when he had been wrestling another boy, bullying him with a painful grip. Suddenly his arms enclosed nothing but the boy's empty clothes, and he fell forward in surprise. The next instant the naked fellow was behind him, had pinned him down and proceeded to choke him unconscious.

That was an initiate's early teleport, just a couple feet and without clothing. Not much, but enough to help when an executioner's pistol is pressed against one's head; enough to jump beyond a cell door.

* * *

Cyan had been an international agent of Evolution. His jobs were in corrupt and crumbling democracies, where he used their own forces against them.

In Canistan to the north the psionics were organized as anti-psi agents working for the government. Somewhat paradoxically, psi drugs were readily available. Even so, Cyan had organized the disruption of a political event wherein one candidate suddenly started speaking gibberish. The prison was brutal.

Mexicorp was different. There the psis were registered, tattoos on face and forearm. By law their households were not allowed to cluster, meaning they were scattered rather than concentrated into ghettos. Psi shield helmets were common for police and government workers. Both sides had compromised Cyan's job there. It was a polite society and the prison was no exception.

Back in the E.R.A., Cyan got medals for both jobs. It was dirty work, but the Evolutionary ends justified the means. Still, now that he was nearing his own death, he acknowledged a couple of betrayals. In one job there was the young man, the idealist he had thrown to the psi cops; in the other job was the woman, his lover, whom he could not ransom.

* * *

On the fourth morning a guard came to take Cyan. The man's face had a look that meant it was not an execution, so Cyan figured it was interrogation. He assumed the physical torture would be as bad as in Canistan, probably worse.

The guard led him out of the psi wing. After a few architectural twists and turns designed to thwart teleports, they came to a brighter building with doors of wood rather than metal: offices of administration.

When they stopped at a door, Cyan readied himself for a tough scene. The guard knocked and a voice bade them enter. The guard opened the door and Cyan stepped into the room where he was surprised to recognize an old friend behind the desk.

"Turk Eyes," he said, dimly aware that the door had shut behind him.

"We meet again," said the man with a smile. He

wore a telepathic shield helmet. "Please sit down."

Cyan took the seat, his mind awhirl. He had been braced for bad, but now a strange new hope began to sprout in him.

"It has been a long time," said Cyan.

"You did me a favor once."

"I tried," he said, giving a dismissive shrug. "It succeeded."

"I do not want you to be shot."

"That makes two of us," said Cyan. "Why exactly do you people intend to have me shot?"

"Listen, Cyan. Listen to yourself. You have separated from Evolution. You say 'you people' instead of 'Evolution.' For the public one needs a trial and legal justification. For us, people of our station, that separation I mentioned should be enough of an answer."

Cyan's seedling of hope was caught in a snap frost.

Looking away, his eye fixated upon a patch on the wall, a square of lighter color. Cyan had seen such a patch at Blue Steel's office a few years before. It was a sign of the change, of the point when jaunters became junkers. Obviously, a picture had hung there for many years, and he knew it had been the first Blue Dream photo. Cyan was in that famous portrait, along with Turk and Blue Steel and True Blue. Twenty-one psionic adepts, from Azure to Zaffer. True Blue had died in his sleep more a decade before, but most of the others had been liquidated over the last few years.

Cyan recalled again the two colleagues he had betrayed: the man through action, the woman through inaction. He closed his eyes and said, "Now I am paying."

"Let me try," said Turk, pressing on. "You are saying that the Evolution I follow, the Evolution of Blue Steel, is not the true evolution."

"Yes, I guess it is as simple as that."

"When did you concoct this idea?"

"Very gradually, during the last few years."

"Let's be more precise," said Turk. "One year? Two? Three?"

"It seems a pointless question."

"I assure you, it is not. I repeat: how long have you been a member of the anti-evolutionaries."

"You know full well that I never joined the anti-evolutionaries."

Turk Eyes sighed and said, "You make me resort to facts." He opened a drawer from which he pulled a stack of files.

"Canistan," he said, flipping through the top file. "Evolution's victory there was almost achieved when suddenly religious dictatorship turned everything over. You were sent there to purge the underground and reorder the ranks. After three months you were arrested, sentenced to two years of prison.

"Those years were hard on you, and it showed. It was expected that you would take a few months to recover at a resort, and then accept some cushy government job, but after two weeks you applied for another mission abroad. Why? Apparently, you no longer felt at ease here. During your absence the country had gone through certain changes that perhaps you did not appreciate."

When Cyan said nothing, Turk continued.

"That is, Evolution discovered the Junker Conspiracy. While the fiend escaped, the other Junkers were liquidated. But they were only the tip of an iceberg, an anti-evolutionary rot of horrific size. You had friends among those convicted and liquidated.

"So, two weeks and then off to Mexicorp. Your progress there was exemplary, yet the rot seems to have followed you. Your two closest agents were recalled under suspicion of anti-evolutionary conspiracy. The investigators established their guilt. You were expected to publicly disavow them, yet you said nothing.

"After six months of this you were yourself recalled. During the second trial, your secretary said you would vouch for her. At that point, remaining mute would look like a confession of guilt. Still you held back until Evolution gave you an ultimatum. Then, with your head at stake, you gave an oath of loyalty, cutting off your lover. You know what happened to her."

Cyan glared at the patch on the wall. Turk sighed.

"You admit to believing for years that we have followed wrong policy, yet I am supposed to believe that you never joined a conspiracy of others. In any case, we hold all the proof."

"Really?" said Cyan. "Then why do you need my confession? Proof of what, anyway?"

"Proof of a planned attempt on Blue Steel's life."

"Do you really believe this, or do you just pretend?"

"You telepaths are so much work," said Turk. "If you were a non-telepath, we could simply have our prober come in and get the answers from you. But look, I will take off my shield and you can do a reading of me."

Turk took off the helmet.

Cyan repeated the question and took a read. Turk was genuinely concerned and did not think the "proof" was real.

Before Turk could put his shield back on, Cyan asked, "What about spontaneous evolution?"

Turk's mind registered a complex tangle of fear and hope.

"Now, now," said Turk, helmet back in place. "I am the one asking questions here. Once, long ago, you convinced me that suicide was petty subhuman stuff. I will see that you do not kill yourself. Then we will be even."

"How is that? Your line of reasoning so far seems to point in the opposite direction."

"We are going to forge a confession," said Turk. "In it you will admit to belonging to a certain group since a specific year, but you will categorically deny planning an assassination—in fact, you will declare you abandoned this group when you learned of its criminal plans."

"No false confessions."

"Shut up and let me finish. Part of this hinges upon whether your case is administrative or public. You understand the difference?"

Cyan nodded. Administrative trials were secret and rather summary.

"For your case to be classed as public," said Turk, "it must have certain features. That is, details fit for public education. Among these is a type of willingness on your part, expressed in the form of a partial confession. Not so different from the loyalty oath. Then we go to trial, where we plea bargain. Realistically you will get a sentence of twenty years, but that really means only two or three years, then an amnesty. So honestly, in five years you are back in society, restored and renewed. Take a few minutes right now to carefully think it over before answering."

"No," said Cyan. "The answer is no. Please have me taken back to my cell."

"Sure," said Turk. He gave a little chuckle. "I didn't think you would agree immediately. Take some time, two weeks. Ask to come back to see me, or send a written declaration."

❃ ❃ ❃

Could Cyan spontaneously develop teleportation power? There was an old theory called "spontaneous evolution" suggesting such a thing: that high stress might cause the psionic mind to evolve new talents. But that seemed impossible, a locker room daydream.

If one found such a skill, how quickly would it develop? Cyan cast his mind back to his psionic testing, in the pre-Evolution days when psionics was illegal and underground. He was a teen at the time, and the testing revealed him to have latent telepathic and ESP abilities. That was a fairly typical combination, since three quarters of all psis had telepathy, and one third of all psis had two talents. Maybe one in ten had three talents. So he might have a sleeping third power that would be awakened under acute crisis.

Then again, the training took a number of months. Would he be allowed to live that long? Probably not.

Cyan tried another pathway: Now that he was being pressured into false confession regarding Blue Wind, might not the "fiend" himself take notice and come teleporting from India to rescue him? He would suddenly appear in the cell beside him. . . and then what? No jaunter had ever been able to carry more than twenty pounds with him, so there was no precedent for jumping out with another person. Maybe Blue Wind could jaunt in with fifteen pounds worth of escape equipment: lock picks, plastic explosives, compact submachine guns. Or maybe Blue Wind had pushed the levels to new heights undreamed of by

Blue Steel, and he could carry another person to the other side of the world.

That seemed too nebulous. Cyan considered the notion of Blue Wind training up an army of jaunters, turning to the logistics of such an undertaking. Blue Wind had been away for a few years. In his first six months he might be able to find and train a lot of new jaunters, but they would be at the naked stage. Cyan wracked his brain for the development curve, and determined it was six years of training to get to the clothing stage, twelve years to get to the loaded stage. So there was no way Blue Wind could have anything more than naked scouts. Unless he had begun years before: thus validating the theory of the Junker Conspiracy as fact.

Cyan laughed bitterly to himself at this irony. Now that he was falsely accused of being in a false conspiracy, he had to pin his hopes upon it being more real than his accusers thought.

* * *

The next day a guard gave Cyan a pencil and some paper, ostensibly for his partial confession. Cyan set them aside for twelve days.

On the thirteenth evening he got a telepathic message:

Good evening, this is 310. We have an execution coming up tonight. Not sure who yet, he is not on our block. Our little tradition is to give our chum a sendoff, drumming on the door as he goes by.

Emotional turmoil edging on nausea blasted through Cyan. "Physical liquidation" had always been an abstraction to him, but now it was close. The prisoner would be led along this corridor, then down to the basement, where a psionic executioner would kill him with a single burst of telepathic assault. No, too romantic: more likely the guards would just shoot him in the back of the head. This is what had happened to the two he had betrayed; this is what would happen to him.

Cyan revolted against the sudden tide of helplessness by trying to figure a way to utilize the psi powers of the other prisoners. He reasoned that the guards could be subject to ghostly tugging and pushing by the TKs within sight, and for longer by the TK-CVs who could follow with ESP. If one could clairvoyantly shadow them down to the basement, he might even jostle the pistol into missing the shot. But to what end? The guard would just shoot again, and the guards knew who all the TKs were among the prisoners.

Only the junkers. A clothed one might teleport in with a silenced pistol and terminate the would-be executioner. A naked scout might blink in, and if he were an expert at weaponless combat, he could silently kill a guard, then don his uniform.

Buoyed by this new concept of scouts with lethal hands and feet, Cyan locked his knees and went into CV mode, leaving his body behind to go clairvoyantly through his door, turn, and walk down the corridor, heading for the next block. He passed through the iron door and, seeing one of the cell doors open, he rushed to look within it. Two guards were there, one mutely reading the sentence aloud to the prisoner. Cyan did not focus on reading his lips since he was curious to see the prisoner, and when the man looked up in silent shouting at the guard, Cyan recognized the face of a hero of SeaTac.

Shocked, he broke his effort and snapped back to his body, where he rushed to vomit into the toilet. He vomited again and again, his stomach a knot of pain, until he heard the drumming in the corridor. He stumbled up and took position at the door. The drumming was louder on the left as the guards approached with their prisoner.

Then they flashed by: two big figures in uniform, dragging between them a third. This hero of SeaTac was now a broken doll, his legs trailing behind him. A bit of garbage being taken out.

It started to seem unreal again to Cyan, but a moment later the prisoner shouted, "Cyan! Cyan!" And Cyan was sick again, knowing that the victim had been used as a prop to get at him.

He slept badly for the remainder of the night. When the overhead light came on in the morning he took up the pencil and started to write his partial confession. While he was self-aware enough to chide himself for having fallen for the one-two punch of Hope and Fear, he put that aside.

"In Year 18 I was approached by an agent of TpF..."

The weeds of Fear began to strangle his garden of Hope: What if Cyan were really just the bait to lure Blue Wind into a prepared trap? What if, now that Cyan was forging a link to the anti-evolutionary, and fervently hoping for rescue by one way or another, he was actually betraying the side he belatedly believed in?

"Their ideology was scientific at first, and I was duped for seventeen months..."

Of course Blue Wind must know that Cyan had been arrested. Even as Cyan reached out toward him, Blue Wind probably probed toward Cyan. If the E.R.A. could locate Blue Wind, that would be disaster enough.

"When at last the TpF removed their mask to reveal themselves as criminals with murderous intent, I directly broke all contact with them..."

Despite his nagging doubts he worked on this project for a day before submitting it to the morning guard to deliver up to Turk Eyes. He thought he would be called to interview immediately, but instead he lingered in limbo for two days.

Two armed guards roused him at two a.m. They marched him down the corridor, then the twisty turns, arriving at the land of offices. Cyan felt his hope rising, anticipating a semi-jocular reception from Turk Eyes, but when the guards opened an office door there was a stranger behind the desk.

Cyan absurdly wondered for a moment if he had been brought to the wrong room. The door closed behind him.

"Sit ya self down," said the man. Cyan realized there was a third person present, a secretary taking notes. He sat down.

"I gots the duty of 'zamining ya while Turk Eyes's away."

"I prefer Turk Eyes."

"Ya gots da right ta make a statement, or ta refuse," said the man. "But in dis here case, seems to me a 'refuse' would take away yer partial confession. Dis would end da 'zamining, an' turn yer case administrative. Ya gets it?"

Cyan nodded. Something had gone bad with Turk, or this was just the "bad cop" switch to throw him off. Either way, he had to act fast.

"I will make a statement."

"Dat's good. Ya inna verra bad spot. I don tink ya really gets how bad it be."

"I will do everything to serve Evolution. Please tell me the accusation in detail."

The man nodded, a smug smile flickering on his lips. He selected a file and handed it to the stenographer. Cyan was bewildered by this, but as the woman began to read the accusation in a flat monotone, he reasoned that having the subordinate do the chore avoided the prospect of the other being exposed as only semi-literate. It would degrade the dignity to have the one in authority stumble over big words; whereas delegating the task served to reinforce the authority.

Cyan bridled at this ignorant hayseed put in power over him. He was a new generation, all right, but he seemed brutish. If this was Evolution, he seemed a step or three backward, nearly subhuman.

Something in the robotic recitation distracted him from his temper: a claim that during his mission in Mexicorp he had begun negotiations with a representative of a foreign power regarding the forceful reinstatement of the pre-Evolutionary regime. Then followed the name of the diplomat as well as the time and place of the meeting. Cyan listened more closely now, and in his memory appeared an insignificant little scene that seemed to match the date. This was clearly the fruit of interrogation of others, but it was such thin gruel that he nearly smiled in relief.

Finally, the stenographer got to the alleged plot to assassinate Blue Steel by way of poison in his afternoon beer.

Then the man said, "Ya done heared da accazation, an' now ya plead guilty."

"No," said Cyan. "You have my partial confession. What I wrote. I will not go along with these ridiculous new charges."

"What ya wrote ain't gonna cut it," said the man. "No way, no how. It's all bullshit, jes' like da las' two times. No more partials for da likes o' you.

Was needed now is a full confession, full o' plans for direct action, not jes' airy egghead 'bad thinkin' stuff.'"

It was tiring for Cyan, which added to the nightmarish quality. After another while of arguing, a new prisoner was shoved into the room. The interrogator asked Cyan if he knew him. Cyan said he looked familiar, but he could not remember.

The man told the prisoner to remind Cyan of where they had met before.

"Cyan coerced me to poison Blue Steel's beer."

"We ain't dere yet, goober. I's axin' where y'all met las' time."

"That was in Mexicorp, where he started me on my terrorist plot against the Evolution's supreme leader."

Cyan remembered the man now, so there was a certain amount of veracity to it, a damning half-truth that was being spun up into a swamp fever fabrication.

The charade dragged on, a daisy chain of lies, half-truths, and absurdities. Cyan nodded off and was woken up to sign the confession. He knew then that he was guilty of killing those other two, the man and the woman, so even if he was innocent of plotting against Blue Steel, his real actions had been worse.

He signed.

Guards walked him back to his cell, a heavenly place lit with morning light, and he fell asleep before his head hit the mattress.

In an hour the cell door opened again. He thought it was breakfast, but no, it was a guard to take him back to interrogation.

This was the pattern for seventy-two hours: long grueling sessions separated by sleep of one or two hours. The pale sunlight at his window might be dawn or dusk. The corridor was always the same.

You are so well informed about my after-dinner conversations in foreign countries, you must know that this one had no consequences. Only 'cuz we done busted ya, jes' inna nikka time. What is Turk Eyes doing these days? In prison he be. What did he do? He botched axin' you. Troof be what's useful to Evolution, lies be what's harmful. We has da right ta invent useful images what da people take for real. Your reasoning here reminds me of the way Turk Eyes thinks. Turk Eyes was over-schooled, like you. I's always tryin' ta use my schoolin' in da service of Evolution. Dat Turk, he was gone bad. 'Was'? Sure, he gots shot las' night. Administrative judgment.

❋ ❋ ❋

For Cyan the rolling back of evolution had gone so far that it was forward again. The original mode of supermen leading the non-psis was still in effect, it had not been compromised. These new supermen were the stage beyond "blue." Did they think of themselves as "indigo"? They had no need for literacy, and what was the point of written words in a telepathic world?

The public trial itself was like a dream. Cyan had plenty of food and plenty of sleep. There were crowds and television cameras. When they asked him whether he pleaded guilty, in a clear voice he affirmed he did. When they asked him if he acted as an agent of the counter-evolution, he again affirmed he did.

It went on like that, but all too soon it was over and he was back in his cell. Once again waiting to be shot.

The door drumming began down the corridor.

Cyan felt befuddled with confusion, since they could not be drumming for him, yet, could they? He forced himself over to the door to drum and watch.

Steps came, slow and dragging. Suddenly his co-defendant entered the range of vision, hands cuffed together behind. He stopped and turned to face Cyan's door. His guard gave an order and he turned to continue his death walk. Cyan saw the guard walk by and then out of range.

The drumming diminished until quiet returned.

A gentle rapping at his door went: tap, tap-tap-tap, tap.

Cyan moved to his window, where he fogged the glass with his breath.

"He did well," said the ghostwriting. "You have ten minutes. How you feel?"

Cyan made a so-so gesture with his hand.

"You will do well, I'm sure. A tip: empty bladder now."

"Don't watch!"

"Ha! I give two minutes . . ."

Cyan used the toilet.

"I will always remember your last girl. Pretty!"

"Yes."

"They coming."

Cyan felt a rush. After a moment, he wrote, "You helped me much. Thanks."

The key snarled in the lock. The door swung open to reveal the guard and a bureaucrat. The civilian pronounced Cyan's name and rattled off the text of a document. They twisted his arms back and put on the handcuffs. He heard the drumming in the corridor.

Cyan led the two down the corridor. There were the steps down to the cellar. Cyan went down, followed by the guard, but the bureaucrat stayed behind.

The stairs were narrow and dark. The drumming had ended. Cyan felt he was backstage now, that an event was over.

At the bottom of the stairs, another corridor. They walked along for several minutes longer than he thought they would.

A dull blow hit the back of his head. There was a breath of peppery smoke. His knees gave and his body made a half turn as it fell. Cyan was wondrous that he felt nothing in the gathering darkness, his cheek against the cool floor.

No junkers. No rescue. Just as well. Fight the good fight.

A vague figure of darkness bent over him, a big pistol hovering close.

A smashing blow struck him on the ear with a roaring silence.

DIGGER'S DAUGHTER, TINY

Digger was a treasure hunter working the mounds of ancient alien cities near his home on Midden World, graveyard of interstellar civilizations. Like most members of this profession, he was squat and strong, rather like the fabled dwarven miners of Earth. Usually he went scavenging for whatever he might find, but on this occasion he was after a specific item desired by an offworld museum (Pan-Human Knowledge House of the Scutum-Crux Arm). Digger happened to know the location of this object (termed "Orb White" by the museum), having seen it once before in the underworld, but the task of retrieving it was too much for him alone, so he enlisted his only child to help out.

Her name was Tiny, but at 5'10" she was too big to be a treasure hunter. Her mother had died in delivering her, and Tiny bore this guilt of having been too big even at birth.

Digger and Tiny were underground at level four. The difficulties of her size had come in the first few levels as they crawled and wriggled through a series of tunnels carved, natural, and burrowed, leaving her with bruises, scrapes, and a new respect for claustrophobia. Then things opened up a bit, and after threading a way with dim lamplight through caverns of mushroom forest and crystal jungle, they had stopped for a meal and a sleep.

Digger woke up as Tiny, bearing a lit lamp, returned to the camp and nearly tripped over the pair of five-foot staves lying on the floor beside her bedding.

Alarmed, he asked, "Where have you been?"

"Nowhere, Papa."

"It is bad, very bad, wandering off. Do not do it again—I mean it."

"Yes, Papa. I am sorry."

Too riled to sleep, he arose and started packing up the camp.

"Poppy?" she said, and he knew there was trouble, so he sat down and waited.

Her cheeks blushed bright red.

"The . . . they . . . we," she stuttered. Then she took a deep breath and started over. "We are racing for the artifact so you can earn a big profit, right?"

"Yes. There is no prize for second place."

"But what if—what if you could win *more* by

losing to the rival?"

Digger exhaled sharply at the notion but then felt his guts knotting up. The "rival" she referred to was young Procyon, the pretentious son of an offworld family that had settled into their town about twenty years before. He was a year older than Tiny, who knew him from school.

Trying to keep his voice level, he asked, "How so?"

"Perhaps the rival seeks a bride and would give you—"

"A bride? Talk straight."

"If the rival gets the item he will give it to you and invest in your business in exchange for your blessing of his marriage."

"My blessing? Who—?"

"His marriage to me."

"Ah." Digger pondered for a moment. "I do not want the 'hows' and 'whys,' I only want to know how much you told him."

"I told him where it is. Where we are heading."

He waited.

"Level Seven," she said. "Three miles northwest of the Corkscrews."

"Ah, everything." Digger sighed with resignation. "Well then, shall we go home now?"

"No, no, we must stay!"

"Why?"

"To make sure he finds it."

Digger shook his head, incredulous. "Must we join his group?"

"Oh no!" she said, her face now pale.

"Explain it to me. I do not understand."

"We will mark a safe trail for them, but remain unseen . . ."

So that is what they did for several hours: beginning with the grotto of the gnomes and ending with the chamber of dancing ghosts, they blazed a path of safe passage. Digger assured Tiny that after the dancing ghosts it was a straight shot to the orb-white.

This strange task irked Digger. Granted he had lost the secret knowledge, the only edge he had in this race, but why should he play the part of a love god for a young man he neither liked nor approved of? It was a mess, but he was trying to make the best of it by going along with his fool daughter.

It was tiring work, so when it was done he set up camp in a little alcove off the dancing chamber. Tiny, full of nervous energy, followed the progress of Procyon's party through the maze.

"They have come," she whispered to Digger.

"Let me rest."

A while later she whispered, "One has started dancing."

"Is it Procyon?"

"No!" she hissed.

"Oh. Let me rest."

Sometime later she shook him awake. She looked upset, so he asked her what was wrong, and she burst into tears.

"Oh Poppy, Poppy, I was wrong. He is a liar and

a cheat, and I am a fool, a fool. I am so sorry."

"Ugh," said Digger, rubbing the sleep from his eyes. "So the wedding is off?"

"Yes. Yes!"

"Then we can try to win the orb ourselves?"

"If there were any hope, but alas, there is none."

"Dry your tears. We will have to take a short cut."

He rustled in his rucksack for a few moments before extracting something small.

"There is some danger ahead, so here, take this." He handed her a locket. "Use it if we get stuck."

* * *

The Sumptuous Gardens of the Birdmen, one of the Sixteen Wonders of the Galaxy, sprawled across the center of the capital city. The human Dilgan Iku was a minor merchant, selling simple booklets of tales, but his kiosk was located near a gate to the Gardens.

"Rosy girls and smiling boys,
Come and buy my little joys.
Tales of Wonder, take a look
Each found inside a little book."

Dilgan took pride in his kiosk. He straightened up the boys' section, their covers with raised swords and desert vistas. He glanced at the girls' section. So different. Here is the one about the girl who could run faster than any man— Dilgan snorted softly and shook his head at the impossibility. Why not make the girl's problem more realistic, like she is too tall? Here is another tale, very popular, where the girl has to be houseguest to a monster man to save her father from death. Such exaggeration!

Dilgan thought of his daughter and her suitor, and grudgingly counted his blessings since the fellow was taller than she, and was not a monster. When would they get married? It could not come soon enough, especially for his wife. These youngsters, dawdling away their time as if they had an endless amount.

The afternoon waned as Dilgan made chit-chat and small sales. The adults, mainly tourists from near and far, came in many exotic shapes and sizes, yet their boys left disorder; their girls were tidy. His daughter came along, looking so professional in her bank teller's dress, signaling that the time had come to close up the kiosk. Another day was done.

As they walked home together, he mentioned his observation regarding stories for girls.

"Oh Daddy," she said. "The girl cannot have a realistic problem because then the reader will just take it as that exact thing."

"Huh?"

"If it is something unusual, then it can stand in for the problem of any girl."

Dilgan thought on that.

They arrived at their apartment where the daughter helped her mother prepare the meal, seeming to take great delight in such a common chore, and then the family enjoyed it together.

A few days later at his kiosk, Dilgan mulled over the growing tension between wife and daughter. Hard to know what it was, except he was caught between them. Well, the daughter wanted to move out, and the mother wanted her to move out, but they had different ideas about that.

When his daughter came to his kiosk at closing time she looked upset. Hoping to distract her or tease the trouble out, he said, "We were talking before, a few days back, about the stories—"

"I want to leave," she blurted. "I want to get out."

Trying for calm, he asked, "Where will you go?"

"I do not know," she said, opening her purse to dig for something, maybe a handkerchief for approaching tears, "But I cannot face that woman again."

"Tonight? Tonight! You will not come home?"

"Here!" she said, thrusting a small object into his hand.

And then the world changed.

One moment he was Dilgan Iku with a kiosk by the Sumptuous Gardens of the Birdmen, with a daughter and a wife, but then he remembered his wife was dead. That she had died in childbirth.

And he was Digger.

"Good job, Tiny," he said, getting his bearings: the cavern, glowing in places with a fungal phosphorescence; the ropey web of sand that had somehow been his kiosk for years or days.

"I am sorry, Poppy. I have ruined it again!"

"Do not cry. What is the matter?"

"That was supposed to be a short cut—"

"It is."

"but to be with mother was too good—"

"Yes, yes."

"and we have been here for many days!"

"No, we have not. Here, look."

He showed her his pocket watch.

"Wait," she said, reading the date window, "it is the same day?"

"Yes. Only hours have passed. Like a dream."

"But the food!"

"Just a dream."

"But—"

"Come along. We must go this way."

"All right, Papa, but tell me about that place."

"From a previous time, an earlier civilization."

"Was it based upon a real place, or an imaginary one?"

"I do not know."

❉ ❉ ❉

They came out of a shrine on top of a hundred-foot high hill, the only elevation in a steppe stretching to the horizon in all directions.

Digger said, "Level Seven."

Tiny gaped. Holding her head, she asked, "Another illusion?"

"That is the question."

"It is so big!"

"Yes and no."

"Can we break the illusion?"

"I do not know. It is not so, ah, 'enchanting' as the last place, but it might be a pocket universe."

Digger looked around at the ground, searching for signs. When he glanced at Tiny he saw her mouth hanging open while she peered at the sky and horizon. He scowled. Then, turning away, he put fingers to his mouth and blew a piercing whistle blast out to the plains. He paused, then blew another to the right, followed by a third to the left.

A galloping sound came to them from down below and he smiled.

After a while a pair of centaurs charged up and stopped, eyeing them warily.

"Hail, runners," said Digger in their language.

The centaurs waited.

"Is Big near here?"

The centaurs looked at each other, then back at him.

"Who art thou?" asked one.

"Me Digger. Me friend Big. Me do favors for Big."

The centaurs led them down the slope to a camp where they presented the humans to their leader, a mighty centaur whose dark beard was streaked with white.

"Ah, little friend," said the leader. "We meet again, to the joy of the Wind Runners. And you have brought another? Much bigger she is. Your mother, mayhap?"

"Hail, hail. This my girl, she call 'Tiny.'"

"Charming. She looks healthy. Methinks a fast runner she must be. No doubt you are proud."

"Thanky, thanky. Me and girl need go River City."

"River . . . ? Oh, yes, I see. Well, you know the way . . ."

"Need go fast-fast."

"Oh. *Oh.*"

❊ ❊ ❊

Digger, requiring speed, had calculated that two pairs of centaurs could alternate in carrying the two humans.

He bargained his best, but all he could get was one youngster to carry them both.

Tiny's height proved advantageous here, as her legs were long enough to get a good grip on the mount's back. But their seating arrangement was difficult: when Digger sat in front, Tiny acted as a chair, and after a while he could see on the horizon the corkscrew towers they were going toward. But Digger bounced a lot, during which his head often struck Tiny's chin. So then they changed the order and he sat behind, where he clung to her in a position even less dignified, and his view was blocked.

As they drew closer to River City, Digger mulled over his current situation. Being a threader of mazes, he tended to apply the same map-making techniques to his own life.

How did I get here? I went after a job, a two-man job, and brought Tiny along because there was no other choice. Have to keep my secrets, since that is all I have, and she is so green she cannot track much. That is what I thought, at least! The reward was all for me, for my retirement or somesuch. But then it went strange, and not in the usual way of traps and monsters, it went goofy in the girlhood, weird in Womandom. What does she want? Who knows! What do I want for her? I do not want her to sell herself too cheap. Gods forbid, I do not want her to be a harlot of the high places, or of the crossroads, for that matter. Along that tunnel path she might instead be a temple dancer — she has got the legs for it, but she is probably a tad top heavy. More against the idea, she shows no interest in dance. My old dream, I guess, but that money went into her schooling instead. Where she rubbed elbows with Procyon.

Digger cleared his throat and said, "You see the corkscrew towers. That is where the rival is coming down."

"They seem to end in the air, like regular towers," she said.

"Yes, just like the hill we came from."

"How can that be, when they connect to levels above?"

"Things are like that here."

He thought, *I should have apprenticed her to a shop, maybe Shell's Millinerium, or even Tobnit's Dry Goods. My fault. Everything is my fault. I have not even a wife to blame.*

My fault for not marrying again, giving her a mean stepmother and then a brood of half-siblings. Instead she had her aunt—

The centaur halted suddenly, bringing Digger out of his meditations. He looked around Tiny's broad back and took in an unusual sight.

Tiny asked, "What is it?"

Their path led down into a depression that had a number of smoking chimney stacks arranged around the perimeter. The stacks looked organic, primordial, as if their knobby stones had grown up from the soil, and the air had a slight sulfurous tinge to it.

With growing unease, Digger answered his daughter, "I do not know."

The centaur was fidgeting, clearly balking at continuing on the path.

"Young one," said Digger, "what is yon smelly things?"

"It is a camp of the walking tree-trunks."

"'Tree-trunks'?"

"Tree-trunk people."

"Where from?"

"From lands below."

"*Below?*"

"What is he saying?" asked Tiny.

"Hush," said Digger. "Young one, just go around."

"No."

"Go around, over by the hungry trees."

"I will not. I must return. Now."

With this the centaur sat his hindquarters down, causing his passengers to slide and tumble off.

Tiny said, "What?"

Digger said, "End of the ride." And then to the centaur galloping away, he called, "Thank you, young one."

Tiny said, "Tell me."

Drawing forth his gas detector, Digger said, "He called this a camp of some outlanders." Digger set the detector on the ground.

"And they leave cook fires burning when they leave?"

"I do not know," said Digger as he bent to retrieve the detector. Glancing at the readout, he did a double take.

"Shall we go through?"

"It is tempting, but no, I want to avoid trouble. We will go around, another way by the hungry trees."

"'Hungry trees'?"

"You will see."

Digger hoisted up his load and led the way to the left. After about a dozen steps he said, "Our friend believes the camp builders came from a level below this one."

"How can that be? Is it even possible?"

"Exactly so," said Digger. The notion of explorers from a subterranean civilization was preposterous. More likely something in a deeper level had woken up: a guardian, a gardener, or a curse. That was an alarming thought, even though it had been many years since anything had erupted to the surface.

Tiny had called the smoking mounds "cook fires," but to Digger they were more like smelters. His gas detector had showed a dangerous level of CO_2 collected in that dimple. Presumably the smoking mounds generated the gas, but creatures breathing something other than oxygen was a puzzler. It suggested intelligent life forms in the pre-oxygen eons of the planet, some sort of 'planimals,' or plant-animals, but it also smacked of time travel from that past.

"Another pocket universe?" she said.

"The notion is less troubling than others."

They hiked in a counter-clockwise sweep on the outskirts of the city center marked by three spiraling towers about three miles away.

They followed a faint animal track that became a path toward a suburb of single story buildings shaggy with thatch roofing. As the pair continued on, they saw human-sized shapes moving among the structures. Tiny drew close to Digger and held his arm.

"Fear not," said he. "They are harmless."

"What are they?"

"Men of dust. They do not talk. They do not see us. If you bump one, he will dissolve a bit, but hardly notice."

"Are they ghosts?"

"Maybe. I think we are ghosts to them."

The path led to a cobbled lane that ended at a circular plot, the hub of the village from which radiated five lanes in spiderweb fashion. At the center of this open area stood a mottled column about nine feet tall, surmounted by a milky sphere around two feet across.

"There it is," said Digger.

They walked around the dustlings until they were beside the column.

While they were shrugging off their rucksacks, she asked, "How shall you get it?"

"You are going up," he said, arranging things on the ground to be ready.

She watched in silence.

Having finished the preparation, he leaned his back against the column and put his hands together to form a step. "You will put your foot here, then stand on my shoulders, and bring it down."

"It looks heavy."

"Please do not drop it on me." He hung some tools on her belt and then she clambered up.

As Tiny was investigating the orb's mounting with her eyes and fingers, Digger saw movement down the first lane to the left, at about ten o'clock: in the middle distance a small cloud of flying creatures crossed from behind one house on the left to another on the right. He thought they were probably frog-bats, a relatively minor nuisance. He had some concern that they were flitting toward the twelve o'clock lane, which was his escape route, leading to the hungry trees.

Tiny tried the wrench, then the pliers.

Digger saw movement on the twelve o'clock lane. It was a party of creatures, the likes of which he had never seen before. From a distance the closest one looked like a big barrel with a long-nosed head on top and stubby legs on the bottom.

Tiny resorted to the crowbar.

The barrel-things saw the humans, watched for a few moments, and then formed a huddle.

"Hurry," said Digger.

Tiny grunted with effort before muttering, "I cannot free it."

"We will switch places if you cannot," he said, in the hope this would spur her to succeed, but instead she climbed down.

"Papa," she gasped as she saw the barrel-things down the lane.

"Yes, we hurry now," said Digger as he climbed up his daughter to stand on her broad shoulders.

Under his feet she trembled with strain as he pried with the bar. The orb moved. A couple more pries would do it.

"Papa, they come."

"Tell me when they are halfway here."

"I shall."

Digger poked and pried again and the orb came up with its mounting flange. He wrapped his arms around the bulk and awkwardly hopped down.

Instantly he sensed there was something odd, something changed.

As Digger lugged the orb to the spot he had prepared, he glanced up the lane to see the barrel-things were now fighting against the frog-bats, but that was not the source of change.

While Digger lashed the orb between the two five-foot staves they had brought, he saw the oddness was closer at hand: the dustlings were all facing Digger and Tiny. The walking dustlings had halted, and other dustlings appeared in doorways and at windows.

When Digger finished his task, the orb was part of a stretcher-like bundle.

"Papa!" cried Tiny, and he saw a burning dustling coming toward them from the left, then another one from the right. A pair of guardians, it would seem.

Digger turned his back on the orb-bundle, crouched and grasped the staff ends.

"Lift up and follow me."

Tiny took up the other handles and started to jog forward with him but she balked as he turned toward the barrel-things.

"Come on!" he shouted.

The barrel-things were still battling the beasts,

but a few turned to track the new sound coming closer. Digger saw that each had four legs and many arms. Their heads were as streamlined as those of birds or sea lions, but there was an unsettling rotted look their faces, as if bones were exposed.

Digger's plan was to dodge and weave through the small crowd to escape the fiery pursuers, but the barrel-things who saw him coming wisely skipped away to one side or the other, even as they swatted at their aerial pests. So the crowd parted, except for one in the middle who was facing the other way, bedeviled by three flapping foes.

Digger dodged around this obstacle so rapidly he nearly tumbled Tiny with torque, but she managed a sidestep gallop through it.

An alien scream of agony erupted behind them. Digger glanced back. The frog-bats were smoldering as they fell. The barrel-thing was falling and the burning dustling emerged from it, barely slowed by going through the living obstacle rather than around it.

Digger ran all out toward the hungry trees. Tiny's longer legs let her drift to the right as if she would come up beside him.

"No!" he shouted. "Stay right behind me. Step where I step."

The hungry trees looked fairly normal, like young pines forty or fifty feet tall, a copse on uneven ground.

Digger heard shouting in his own language.

Glancing over his shoulder he saw Procyon and team chasing the burning dustlings. The young man was waving a shiny rod like a sword.

"Turn left!" Digger cried, and he steered Tiny into a tight curve.

She stumbled as the ground beside her opened like a gaping mouth, exposing a deep gullet with crumbled bones at the bottom. For an instant she teetered at the brink, but Digger's drive tugged her to safety.

Once again the burning one made a beeline toward them, this time falling into the pit.

The mouth snapped shut, then convulsively opened and shut with hissing and smoke coming out.

In the center of the copse of hungry trees stood a thing like an elegant teacup grown to the size of a card table. Digger halted before this object and panted, bent over.

Looking back the way they had come, he saw the second burning dustling was down but still crawling toward the orb with one leg, until Procyon hacked away an arm with the silver rod. Recognizing the rod, Digger shook his head in disbelief. It was a common artifact of the towers, called a dowsing stick, and was usually ignored for being nearly worthless. With this unlikely weapon Procyon chopped at the flaming foeman's neck and the creature popped like a log in the fireplace, dissolving to embers.

"Tiny," called panting Procyon as he ran over,

adroitly dodging the mouths. "*Scintilla,* darling, thank the gods you were not harmed."

Digger was so shocked that the rival knew his daughter's private name that he ignored the implication of the other words. Numb, he glanced at the two guides and nodded to them with professional courtesy. They nodded back.

"Yes," said Digger to Procyon, finding his voice. "Thank you for your help. That was a surprise, I will admit. Here, take up this end, then you and she can carry it into the cup there."

"Gladly," said the young man. "My, it is heavy. Surprisingly so."

After they had set down the awkward orb-load so that it stood on its staff ends, Digger pushed in behind them so that all stood in the narrow cup. With his back to the hired men, Digger told the couple that the cup would carry the three of them through all levels and leave them on a hill a few miles from their town. The hired guides would walk back home from the hungry trees.

Then Digger activated the artifact. It lifted an inch, then settled back down.

"Must be too much weight," said Digger, his heart sinking.

It was plain what he must do. The orb would be the wedding present for the couple. Or they would fight over it on the hilltop. It was between them.

Digger stepped off, but before he could offer any words he was bowled over by Procyon's tackle, and then the teacup shot up into the sky.

"What are you doing?" cried Digger, his fist clenched for a fight. "I was getting off!"

"I did nothing! She shoved me!"

Incredulous, Digger looked at the shrinking teacup for a moment, then he laughed heartily.

"It is not funny!" said Procyon, as the teacup disappeared. "When will the cup return?"

"It will not," said Digger, drying his eyes. "A new one will grow. It takes a few days, maybe. We are walking back. No prize for second place, but we can probably find some valuable items on our way out."

The young man scoffed, but then seemed to realize that he had no other option. He sketched a rueful smile, and Digger was surprised to feel that maybe Procyon was an all right fellow after all.

SPECULATIVE ENVOY

The small lecture hall had tier seating on risers so steep that the steps seemed nearly rungs on a ladder. The susurrating audience occupying the tiers exhibited all the shades of selenium toning: white, black, and gray. Into this softly buzzing room entered an administrator, followed by an exotic guest.

"Silhouettes, shadows, and images, come to order," said Prefect Reflect. "The stranger beside me has come to visit. No doubt this is the first meeting for all of us, and probably the first visit in centuries. Allow me to set this moment within context.

"Of late there has been friction between the Others and ourselves. The Others claim that we are violating the Treaty of Strict Imitation, that some of our members are not reflecting with proper deference and decorum. They express a fear that we grow too powerful, and will launch another war. Needless to say, neither side of the Glass wants war. In an effort to reduce tensions, we must study diligently.

"To further this aim, an envoy has been sent to us from the Otherside. He will introduce himself and his people. Please welcome Mr. Gordon Phillips."

"Hello, Mirror-folk," said the stranger. "My name is Gordon Phillips. I come from Rancho Mirage, which is near Los Angeles in the Real World. I have studied your language and can speak it, a little. I came here by way of a full-length mirror, and believe me, entering was the most difficult part."

He paused for a reaction, only to be met with pin-drop silence. Mildly anxious, he continued:

"The first place I found was of course the reflection of my own room. I struggled there for a while before I realized that I could not open the door, and that I must try to move at right angles, so I slipped sideways and entered the Silver Plains.

"Eventually I found myself in the dim and uncharted regions of your home territories. I am proud to be here, and very excited about this meeting. Now then, are there any questions?"

An argent image in the front row raised a flickering hand.

"Yes?" said Gordon, disconcerted as the other's face flickered between chrome gray and a reflection of his own visage.

"How old are you?"

"Twenty-six," said Gordon. The room erupted with laughter. Gordon looked to the Prefect, who shrugged apologetically.

"Forgive them for their immaturity. As you can tell, our acoustics are rather flat . . ."

"Tinny," said Gordon.

"We prefer 'silvery,' but yes, you see my meaning. In any event, the words 'six' and 'sex' are virtually identical. Keep this in mind. And be aware that the sum of twelve and twenty-four will disrupt the class to no end."

"I see. Thank you, Prefect." This was the first check: the setting was not as august as he had originally thought.

He asked if there were any other questions.

A shambling shade of smoky pearl lowered its extended pseudopod.

"Erawrevlis esu uoy nac?"

"'Erawrevlis'?"

"Sey."

"The question is, 'Can you use silverware?' and the answer is yes, I use it every day in the Real World."

The audience broke into applause.

"Mr. Philips, you speak our language so well!" gushed a comely silhouette.

"No, no," said Gordon, modestly. "Really I am quite poor at it."

"I am impressed by your familiarity with

Silverware," said Prefect Reflect. "It is the essence of our culture, if you will." Gordon looked slightly bewildered, so he added, "We shall speak of this later. More questions for Mr. Phillips?"

The questions continued, most of them silly, some of them interesting, and a few of them baffling. One insight that surprised Gordon was the hatred that the inhabitants of specula held for electricity, which they seemed to think of as some kind of god.

"Bring back the night," said one inky shadow. "You Others are working us twenty-four hours a day, working us to death. Is it any surprise that we tire too easily now? The wrinkles and gray hairs you see are not yours but our own, yet we hear complaints that we are somehow rebelling or straining the treaty."

This was the second check. Gordon could sympathize, but then again, the mirror people had invaded the Real World one night in China circa 2600 B.C. As long as the towns and cities held back the night with a luminescent grid, the power of the mirror folk would be curbed.

While Gordon was answering the question, a flicker of movement caught the corner of his eye. He glanced out the window at a flitting shape of unworldly colors: tint of birdsong in rain; hue of acidic bitter flavor; tinge of ribbed texture; and shade of malodorous stench. He felt an icy chill take his heart.

This was the third check.

He managed to finish his sentence, but his mind was racing along another track. *Dear God, that was the Fish! It has awakened. The treaty* has *been broken. It must be true, then, that they killed that Jesuit in Canton, back in 1736. What was his name, Pinocchio? No, Fontecchio! Perhaps the Fish itself crossed over and killed him!*

Just as suddenly, Gordon saw that they knew that he knew. There would be no easy return to the Real World, at least while living. He decided to make the session last as long as possible, afraid of what was bound to happen next . . .

Too late! With a pounce, the Fish was upon him. As the tiger tongue looped around Gordon's body, he knew he was the first casualty of a new war; as he was drawn into the churning maw, he knew he was the fool who had accidentally triggered the invasion by showing the path; as he died the Fish leaped into Los Angeles, followed by a storm of the age old enemies.

Within twelve hours, the rest of the planet was engulfed in a war of extermination.

It did not end well.

VITAMIN DOUBLE-D

T his is one of those stories where a city
slicker has to run a farm.

Ocie Odie gripped the bus seat ahead of
him with white-knuckle intensity. The vehicle was
not plunging off the Golden Gate Bridge, it was
only moving north, away from his hometown
of San Francisco. Silently the twenty-something
cursed his fate, that his day job as a data entry clerk
had been outsourced to Nigeria. His desperate
need for a paycheck had pushed him beyond his
comfort zone, and he was leaving the City for a job
lead suggested by his mother regarding an "uncle"
with temp work out in the hick sticks. Pay was
under the table.

He noticed how a child sitting beside his
grandmother in the side-facing seats ahead looked
at Ocie's grip with a puzzlement that became

concern. Ocie felt ashamed that the next county over was as alien to him as flyover country, and he pledged he would try to see it as the farmlands outside Paris or Milan. Having done this, Ocie forced himself to release, and rested his sweating hands on his thighs clad in high-fashion denim.

You see, our city slicker Ocie was a metrosexual with just enough common sense to know that a grass skirt, one of the best ways to show off perky nipples, was No Go for dairy work. So he wore a pair of Barbarella Jeans: their clear plastic domes showed off his knee-pulls, a rosy pair of Raised American Beauties surgically grafted onto his knees.

The bus went deeper into rural Marin County until finally Ocie Odie reached his stop. He unloaded his bicycle from the holding rack in front and rode a few miles, past a farm of some kind, and then a ranch of free-range ostriches, the mere sight of which made his stomach growl.

At last he arrived at the Double-D dairy farm. The place had a small parking lot facing the front office, but Ocie did not see a bicycle hitching post, so he followed the service road around the back. With surprise he discovered a much bigger parking lot fronting a barn-like structure and a smaller, one-story building to the right. Next to the front office stood a secure rack, where he locked up his bike.

He went in the back door of the front office, calling out. The place, reassuringly office-like, was empty of people.

He shrugged, went back out the door, and started across the empty parking lot toward the buildings. A chunky woman with green hair emerged from the smaller structure, yawning and rubbing the sleep from her eyes. She livened up when she saw him, and hurried over in a jiggling jog.

"May I help you?" she asked. He guessed her to be twenty-two, a few years younger than himself.

"I'm here for the job," he said. He felt some pity for her as a rural. She was obviously reaching for fashion with that hair color, but she was obese as most country people.

"Oh!" she said. "Uncle said you'd be here. Thank you so much for helping us on such short notice." She lowered her gaze toward the ground, almost a bow, but then she stiffened and burst out, "Oh no, what happened to your knees?"

Ocie Odie sputtered with indignation.

The woman's eyes widened, then she tittered and blushed. She blushed more deeply and tore her eyes away. "Pardon my surprise," she stammered, her eyes flicking across his head from ear to ear, as if struggling to make eye-contact. "I've heard of this, but I've never seen . . . They're lovely—handsome!"

"Thank you," he said with an edge of frost.

"Please call me Sissy," she said. "Everybody does." She used a megawatt smile to melt his ice, and then she proceeded to show him the ropes for operations at the front office. Filing cabinet. Delivery schedules, pick up schedules, bookings for the petting zoo. Landline. The various scripts to use when dealing with telephone calls. At one point she made a comment that Uncle was in China on business.

Another corpulent woman entered the office.

"Jun," said Sissy, "this is Mr. Ocie Odie, managing for Uncle. Mr. Odie, this is Jun. She's a sort of captain."

"Pleased to meet you," said Jun, offering her hand. She was brunette and a few years younger than Sissy.

"Nice to meet you. Please call me Ocie, not this mister stuff."

Sissy frowned. Jun simpered and said, "Yes . . . Ocie."

Sissy said, "Jun, go fetch Miyu so she can meet Mr. Odie. And then get to work—look how late it is!"

"Yes ma'am," said Jun. "Goodbye Mr. Ocie." She spun on her heel and left the room.

"Discipline will suffer," said Sissy, shaking her head.

"But—"

"You know, I hate to ask, but, are you . . . lactose intolerant?"

The question came from nowhere, baffling Ocie Odie. Was it a joke? He decided it must be "legal," so he said, "No."

"Not that it matters, of course, with you in the

front office here, but still, there might be health issues. Except there won't be, because now we know, and you won't be in contact anyway."

A heavy young blonde woman burst into the room. She had two high-mounted ponytails, like drooping bunny ears.

"Hello Mr. Ocie Odie, I'm Miyu—wow, look at those knee-pulls! What a pair! American Beauties, am I right? Super stylish. Pygmy Gumdrops are too small, Flapjacks are w-a-a-ay too big, but Beauties are just right! The bee's knees, like Benny Lava." Miyu started doing a little hula dance, waving her arms and singing "'Polka-polka, pol-ka. Polka-polka, pol-ka.'"

"*Miyu*," said Sissy with some severity, but Ocie found himself charmed.

"'Who put the goat in there?'" he sang, sketching Bollywood gestures with his arms. "'The yellow goat I ate?'"

"Mister Odie, please!" said Sissy.

Miyu doubled over laughing but then recovered to stand straight and semi-serious, the mischief in her eyes signaling she was ready for more. As fun as it was, Ocie felt a twinge that he was being unprofessional, so he sobered up as best he could.

"Yes, Sissy. I'm sorry—I got carried away."

"I understand," said Sissy with a motherly smile. "Our little Miyu is quite spirited. Now, please forgive me, but I really must check on the work. Miyu, please behave."

"Yes ma'am," she said, making a little curtsy.

"I'll be back in a few minutes," said Sissy as she went out the door.

Ocie turned to Miyu and said, "So are you going to help me learn my new job here?"

"I sure will!"

"Any pointers so far?"

Miyu screwed her face up in cloudy concentration for a moment, then brightened and snapped her fingers. "I know, you've got to get the mail. Come on, I'll show you."

She led him out the front door, and after pointing to the mailbox over by the road, she hooked her arm with his, invading his personal space. While this blitzkrieg contact caused him some alarm, she acted as if it were the most natural thing in the world, somehow suggesting she was infirm, as if she might trip on a crack or something.

Ocie cleared his throat and asked, "Shouldn't you be in school?"

"But I *am* in school."

"You mean, you're here as part of a class?"

"No, this is my school, all day, every day."

As they walked, she was slightly behind, which made him like a shield she was using against unseen dangers. Ocie Odie had thus been thrust into a role, of walking cane and protecting shield, helper and defender—guardian. This caused unusual feelings in his chest, a mixture of confusion and pleasure. He was a knight, and she, a damsel. To counter such atavistic daydreams, he continued asking her probing questions.

"Did you take the GED?"

"What's that?"

"It's a test so you can quit high school early."

"High school!" said Miyu. "I love those uniforms."

"Uniforms?"

"Sure!"

There was at times a gentle pressure on the back of his upper arm, a warm pillow that made him feel useful and contented, but then with a shock he realized what it was, and how the young woman was using this more intimate contact to steer him, in the same way a rider directs her horse through pressures of her knees. This downgrading of his self-image from "knight" to "horse" sobered him a great deal.

"So how many milk maids are here?"

"A dozen."

"Wow, so many. And how many cows?"

"Um, a dozen—say, Mr. Odie, what kind of birds are those? Are they larks, or finches?"

Ocie examined the birds on the wire. Their breast feathers were speckled, like unblinking eyes.

"I don't know," he said, "but those over there are crows."

They arrived at the mailbox and retrieved its contents: a few bills, an odd catalogue, and a couple of advertisements. The birds on the wire fled, chased away by a gray bird with black stripes on its wings. This invader burst forth in song, but after one phrase, it abruptly switched the song into another for a few seconds, followed by the sound of a telephone ringing.

"Wow," said Ocie as they started walking back.

"It's a mockingbird," said Miyu, giving a sniff of disapproval.

"It seems so . . . mechanical." He looked down at her face and asked, "How old are you, Miyu?"

"Really?" she asked, glancing around conspiratorially.

"Really."

"Twelve."

Ocie jumped.

"'Twelve'? How is that possible? I mean, you— you're so—big!"

"We drink lots of milk."

"Well that doesn't mean any—wait a sec, what kind of milk?"

"Cow milk, silly."

"From your own cows?"

"No, no—never!"

"So maybe you are drinking milk laced with growth hormones."

"Sure, that's what makes us big."

Ocie was lost in thought, running down the threads of a conspiracy. Big Milk. The filthy greedy corporations used growth hormones to increase milk production. Even though the growth hormones were present in the milk, they always claimed that it had no effect on human consumers of the milk, yet here was "smoking gun" proof: the maturation of a pre-teen girl, such that she looked many years older. All at a rural lab, far from prying eyes. But why would a filthy greedy corporation do that, other than because it was cheaper and more evil?

"What does Sissy think about this?"

"She drinks it herself. I mean, look at her! Making like an adult when she's only seventeen—oops! Don't tell her I told you! Promise?"

"Yeah, I promise."

"Pinkie promise?" She held out her fist with the little finger extended.

"What do you mean?"

"You link them, and shake."

Just as they completed this action, Sissy stormed out the front door and hurried toward them. Ocie felt Miyu stiffen, but then she pushed herself more firmly into the back of his arm. Behind them the mockingbird was ringing again.

"Miyu," said Sissy, her voice aquiver. "Let go of Mr. Odie's arm."

"But why?"

"Because he is not a guest," said Sissy. "He is . . . staff."

At this precise moment the singing mockingbird overhead began crying like a baby. All at once Ocie felt wetness against the back of his arm and saw two growing spots of moisture appear on Sissy's blouse.

"Wha-what?!" he stammered, thinking she had been shot. Miyu let go of his arm and began moving away.

"It's that cry," said Sissy, crossing her arms to hide the wetness. "It triggers . . . ahem, spontaneous letdown."

Miyu dashed around the corner of the front office as Ocie's mind went into a whirl. With a jolt he realized that both teenage girls were leaking milk. This in turn meant that both were mothers, a shocking revelation. The place was therefore some sort of home for teen moms, or a baby farm, or something run by religious fundamentalists.

But at the same time he felt a storm of long suppressed emotions in the form of memory chains. One chain had several links: in the first he learned breast-feeding was for babies; in the next he rejected the breast, proudly declaring he was not a baby; and yet in the third link came a burning jealousy when he saw his younger brother nursing at the magical mounds that were once his property, and his alone. Another chain illustrated Ocie's further isolation from breasts, as endowed females began hugging him in a reserved way, at a distance, like a makeup preserving air kiss, but here to withhold contact with their upper bodies. The Forbidden Zone. For infants only.

❆ ❆ ❆

Coming out of his fugue, Ocie Odie found himself

in the office, alone. Brunette Jun came in, looking slim. Ocie realized with a start that her bust was less pronounced than before.

"How embarrassing," she said with a soft sly smile, "that a loud bird caused a few leaks."

"I was surprised! I guess the bird learned that cry from your babies in the back?"

She came up short, giving him a blank look.

"We don't have any babies."

"You mean, they aren't here?"

"No, I mean we haven't had any," she said. "In fact, the point is, we're all virgins."

"But how—?"

"What," she said with a sneer, "you thought this was some kind of baby farm? Home for disgraced girls?"

"I guess so," said Ocie Odie, his face burning. "I'm confused. Are there . . . are there any cows here?"

"We are the 'cows.'"

❋ ❋ ❋

Ocie Odie found himself in the office restroom. The door was locked. The nipples on his knees were looking up at him accusingly. He apologized to them, but he wasn't sure why.

Then it hit him. For the first time, he saw beneath all the post-modernism, post-modemism, irony, and surrealism, like layers of an onion. In a thunderbolt of revelation he saw that the knee-pulls were an expression of what he could only term "boobie envy." He felt his face blazing hot with shame, that he had never seen it before, and what it seemed to say about him.

But it was not really envy. He had mutilated himself to show that he desired women, transforming himself into exactly the type of quasi-hermaphrodite the cruisers found repulsive. It was an armor against amor unwanted; a garland of garlic to keep the suckers away.

Meanwhile, back in the world, Sissy was begging Ocie through the door to talk to someone on the phone. That seemed reasonable, so he went out. Sissy handed the receiver to him before giving him privacy by walking out the back door.

"Ocie, this is Uncle. I apologize for not contacting you sooner—this big thing came up, and just got bigger. Anyway, I'm sure you have lots of ideas about the farm, and most of them are probably wrong, so let me tell you the whole thing to set you straight. Okay?"

"Okay."

"All right. Now, you know about China's one child policy?"

"*China?* Well, sure."

"Good. And how they all want boys?"

"Uh, I guess so. I mean, I can see how—"

"And that means they don't want girls."

"Sure."

"So the girls all go to orphanages. And I rescue them, bring them to the States. For two reasons

—first because it is good to help them, and also because those pampered princes of China are going to be lacking brides. So the dairy farm is also a bridal finishing school."

"Wait a second," said Ocie, "there are no babies here."

"That's right, the little ones are in homes until they hit puberty."

"You boost them with something so they produce milk."

"That's right—we avoid the falsity of implants and cosmetic surgery, and the secret is that a lactating woman actually matches the template of attraction. She has the big boobs, of course, but she also has a slim waist. See, men are programmed to be drawn to such a female. She has proven to be fertile, and she is at her most beautiful."

"But these girls haven't had babies, right? So that part is a lie, almost up there with implants."

"Maybe so, but that's a plus, not a minus," said Uncle. "I mean, their virginity ain't a secret, it's a prized condition. What we're selling is milk of virgins."

That gave Ocie pause. It sounded like a New Age term.

"You still there?"

"And the milk goes to. . .?"

"Clients. High paying subscribers."

"So it's not going to the Milk Bank."

"No, never."

"Not sold at convenience stores?"

"Nope."

Ocie ran it through his mind for a few moments.

The place was not a baby farm, nor a cult-based shelter for teen mothers; it was a human milk dairy, populated by rescued girls. Almost certainly a New Age deal. He could imagine that virgin milk was more organic than organic for a certain crowd of discerning caregivers for infants. The girls seemed happy, and healthy, once one recalibrated for such curves as they possessed. True, they had some sort of body modification done to them, but then, he himself had body mods on his knees.

"Well, okay."

"Great! I'm glad we had this talk. And thanks again for your hard work!"

Ocie did the office work until the day was done, then he clocked out, rode his bike to the bus stop, and got on the bus. Things looked different—no, people looked different. He went home, went to sleep, and when he woke up things were back to normal.

Ocie found himself in a bit of a fashion crisis. The mini-kilts, while more business-like than grass skirts, were simply No Go. As were meggins. He put on the "barbs" again, with a fresh shirt that was slightly more casual than the one before.

Back at the Double-D, Ocie arrived during a mechanical crisis: the breast pumping machine was broken. Sissy had called in for a new unit, but it would not arrive for many hours; in the meantime, milking would have to be done somehow.

There was a single hand pump device, but the girls had no experience with it.

"It sounds like a math problem," said Ocie, licking his lips nervously. "I'm no good at math, but explain it to me slowly so I can get a grip on this."

Problem: normally each girl pumped eight times a day. Pumping takes ten minutes. Ten minutes times twelve girls equals two hours, at which point it is time for the first girl to pump again.

Ocie's head was swimming. Eight times a day?! Every two hours?! These girls were athletes!

The hand pump was like a sprayer bottle that drew in rather than spraying out. Sissy volunteered to be first. After some awkwardness, Ocie managed to get it in place upon her swollen breast, and before long he got into the rhythm of it. Even so, it took nearly an hour to drain Sissy.

Next it was Jun. Ocie pumped her out in about forty minutes. His hand was getting tired.

Third up was Miyu. She seemed sort of feverish, in contrast to her high energy of the day before, and her bust seemed extra large. Miyu seemed relieved after the first few minutes, but Ocie's hands were cramping. Sissy and Jun massaged his hands, while a revitalized Miyu tried pumping herself for a while.

When the replacement pump finally arrived,

Ocie thought he was done.

"Oh no," said Sissy. "We have a backlog now." So as the machine began processing the nine unpumped girls at its usual pace, Ocie pumped Sissy again.

"I feel like John Henry," he said, getting drunk on fatigue. "I'm competing against a machine!"

Sweat getting into his eyes, he pumped Jun again.

"All this math!" he said. "So you lose nearly a cup size when you are drained. Well, it makes sense! And a D cup is a ratio of four inches bigger than the band size—I never knew that, the relation of the letters to inches, and the ratio."

They massaged him, they praised him, they answered his questions. He grew determined that they should learn to handpump themselves—it was important for them to be self-reliant.

They broke for lunch but were back at it by one o'clock.

When he quit for the day, his hands were so worn out it was difficult to hold the timecard to punch out. On his bike, his hands could barely grip the handles, and squeezing the brakes was so difficult that instead he dragged his feet on the ground to stop. On the bus, people looked different —no, women looked different. At a glance he automatically determined their cup size.

He went home, went to sleep, and dreamed he was a minotaur protecting his herd of milkmaids from a stampede of frenzied ostriches.

* * *

The third morning was relatively uneventful compared to the day before. Ocie was in his office, the girls were in their dorm. Order had been restored.

At the end of the day as he was getting ready to leave, Ocie received a phone call from Uncle. After thanking Ocie for dealing with the pump breakdown, and praising him for his gumption in that endeavor, Uncle got to the point: "Ocie, I need your help. I know it isn't in your job description, but there's a quick plumbing job—"

"Plumbing? Oh no, I can't—"

"It's quick and easy, just clearing out a drainage line that's probably clogged with hair—women, right? So Sissy will show you the tools and some work clothes you can change into, okay?"

"But—"

"Great!"

Sissy gave Ocie Odie a stack of clothes, which he dutifully took into the restroom. He emerged in a red sweatshirt beneath a pair of denim overalls, with a pair of oversized work boots on his feet. He asked for some kneepads to protect his knee-pulls and she found him a pair. He resisted wearing the workman's cap until she mentioned spiders and cobwebs getting into his hair.

Ocie would not dare wear such an ensemble in frisky San Francisky, since it was so close to the "handyman" look that the cruisers would proposition him at every turn.

"This is your tool kit," she said, hauling over a plastic bucket loaded with a variety of mysterious items. "Here's the plunger, the hand snake, the wrench, the duct tape, the flashlight—that's important! And here are some rags to put in your pocket."

"How do I use the snake?"

She showed him.

Sissy led him from the office across the parking lot to the barn. Inside this structure, Ocie found a cavernous, half-lit room that felt nothing like a barn, but more like an empty movie set, or a museum area cleared for a new exhibit. They went straight through to a door that opened onto another big room, but this dim chamber looked like a movie set of a barn, having a short fake yard of hard dirt and a rickety old half-barn. They crossed the ersatz outside, entered the gloomy barn, and went through to the back where a door opened onto a little metal stairway up to another door, that in turn opened into the interior of a 19th century European train car.

Ocie again got the feeling he was viewing a museum exhibit, or the private collection of an eccentric billionaire, as they walked down the glass-lined corridor, passing four compartments on the left, each opposite a station door on the right. They exited through a door marked "Cabinet," descended another flight of metal steps, and ended at a heavy wooden trap door in the concrete floor.

"Good luck," she said. Ocie tried to lift it, but could not.

Together they strained, and then it was up, and he went down.

Bent over, he followed the flashlight beam along the access tunnel that seemed to go at a right angle to his trip through the barn/stage complex, putting him beneath the dorm. There were dusty webs and occasional drips, making him glad for the cap. After crouch-walking for a surprisingly long way, he found the drain clean out.

Applying the tool to it, he quickly wrenched his wrist and busted his knuckles. Some eye-popping strain later he managed to remove the cover. Stagnant water came out. He put the bucket in place too late. Ocie took up the snake and put the head of the flexible steel cable into the open pipe. He continued feeding it in until it met resistance, then he tightened the snake lock and began turning the disk-shaped crank. The augur head bit into something and pulled him forward. He kept cranking but the head was stopped, so then he released the lock and reversed-cranked it. Through the cable he could feel he was pulling something along, like a fisherman reeling in a big catch. At last he drew forth a rat-sized clot of tangled hair.

"And that's why they call it a snake," he said to himself, "because it gets the rat."

Ocie Odie felt a novel sense of

accomplishment. His muscles were sore, his back ached, his wrist felt broken, and there were scabs on his knuckles, but as he tightened down the drain cleanout cap, and coiled up the snake, he felt good.

Even so, as he walked his hunched-over way back down the tunnel, something broke inside Ocie Odie, releasing a flood of conflicting emotions that swept aside all the careful reasoning he had accepted before. He vowed to have his knee-pulls removed. With heady indignation he saw the whole dairy farm project as exploitative, degenerate, and degrading. It was human trafficking, and once he told the authorities, then things would be set right.

When he got to the tunnel entrance, he found a far different scene than when he had left. There was the noise of heavy machinery moving something massive. As he climbed up, an executive bodyguard swore in French and halted him. Ocie saw a lot of people around, all security or stage techies. There was a techie glued to a video monitor showing a movie of a train ride by the coast.

The guards were arguing with the techies about this plumber screw-up. The techies were saying it was fine, he would just walk through the train car on their cue. Just as Ocie was about to ask a question, the techies hustled him up the stairs to the swaying train door and pushed him in.

* * *

An old-fashioned conductor stopped him just inside the car that was rocking as if it were moving down a railroad at a fast pace. The illusion of motion was compounded by the windows that showed landscape moving past—they appeared to be traveling along the coast of the French Riviera, above the Mediterranean, late in the day. The air in the car was scented with the perfume of Riviera summer, sun-baked orange and roses, completing the illusion.

The car had only two passengers, who faced each other in the third compartment. The conductor took Ocie by the arm and advanced slowly until they had a good view.

The passenger facing them was the milkmaid Jun, dressed as a young peasant woman wearing a white bonnet and puffy white blouse. The other passenger was a balding man with glasses, in the scruffy clothes of an itinerant worker or vagabond. They sat silently as the train swayed and the landscape flashed by. The sun was sinking into the sea, and a fishing boat sat there as if asleep, reflected in the blue water.

The atmosphere was warm and hypnotic, but Jun seemed distressed, almost feverish. Her hair lay damp upon her forehead, and tiny beads of sweat glistened above her upper lip. Breathing with difficulty, she started fumbling with her blouse, unlacing it, opening it up, exposing her left shoulder.

She said something in French, and the man answered in hesitant affirmation.

The scruffy man knelt before her, taking off his glasses. She brought out her left breast, huge, tight, tipped with a strawberry, and he took it reverently into his mouth. He drew deeply. She sighed in relief, her head leaning back to tap against the glass pane. She seemed to almost fall asleep.

A minute or two passed. The conductor suddenly twitched, as if coming awake in alarm, and shoved Ocie forward toward the door marked "Cuisine." As Ocie was passing their glass door, Jun stirred and said something. The bald man switched to the other breast, and with a shock Ocie recognized the President of France.

❈ ❈ ❈

Leaving the French train, he was halted by security agents in the dark barn, with the sound of rain beating down and a cold dampness in the air that made him sneeze. He noticed a calendar for 1939 hanging on a nail just before he was handed over to a techie who whispered, "You got to go straight through, you get it? On my go." Ocie thought this place was violating the fire code by not having more exits, but he held his tongue.

He took in the stage dressings: rusty farm

tools lying on the dirt, an iron wheel, a broken thingamajig, and a plow with a disk. Rain seemed to hammer on the roof, and dripping streams formed a curtain at the entrance.

By that far doorway, Ocie saw a bunch of rain-bedraggled Oakies: a matriarch, a young woman, and two children. Movement in the near corner revealed a black man on his back, and a boy sitting beside him. The boy got up slowly and went toward the wet ones, asking, "You own this here?"

"No," said the crone, "jus' come in outta the wet. We got a sick girl." She gestured to the young woman, who was Miyu. "You got a dry blanket we could use an' get her wet clothes off?"

The boy returned to the corner, fetched up a dirty comfort, and brought it to the crone.

"Thank ya," she said. "What's the matter'th that fellah?"

"Fust he was sick—but now he's starvin'!"

"What?"

"Starvin'. Got sick in the cotton. He ain't et for six days."

The crone walked over to the corner and looked down at the man. The boy drifted beside her.

"Your pa?"

"Yeah," said the boy. "Says he wasn't hungry, or he jus' et. Allays give me the food. Now he's too weak. Can't hardly move."

The sound of rainfall let up to a soothing swish on the roof, the thick streams at the door weakened into strings of drops. The gaunt man moved his lips. The matriarch knelt beside him and put her ear close. His lips moved again.

"Sure," she said. "You jus' be easy. He'll be awright. You jus' wait'll I get them clo'es off'n my girl."

The crone moved to Miyu, holding up the comfort to screen her. "Now slip 'em off." When she was naked the crone folded the comfort around her.

"He's dyin', I tell you!" said the boy. "He's starving to death."

The crone's eyes passed Miyu's eyes, and then came back to them. And the two women looked deep into each other. The girl's breath came short and gasping. Ocie saw she was in the same sort of no-kidding physical distress afflicting Jun in the train, the same state Miyu had been in the day before, when the pumping was late.

"Yes," said Miyu.

"I knowed ya would," said the matriarch, glowing with pride. "I knowed!"

She turned to the boy, saying, "Hush. Come on, you fella. You come out in the shed for a time."

They left, crone and children like a hen with three chicks. Miyu stood still in the whispering barn, then she drew the comfort around her and moved slowly to the man.

Slowly she knelt down beside him, loosened one side of the blanket, and bared her breast. He shook his head weakly.

"You got to," she said, bending low. She drew his dark head up to meet her flesh. "There. There."

A techie pushed Ocie and he made his way quietly through the barn, past the tableau with Miyu and the American president.

❊ ❊ ❊

The next room had Chinese bodyguards. The air was hot and humid, with traces of oriental incense. Upon seeing the brown woodwork like a cage around the raised bed with canopy, Ocie gasped with recognition, remembering his trip to Beijing. This set was a recreation of the Imperial bedroom from the Forbidden City. Reclining on the bed, a man swaddled like a baby beside a woman in black, her green hair bound back, her full breasts exposed, heavy with milk. She softly sang what sounded like a Chinese lullabye. It was a tableau from Bertolucci's movie *The Last Emperor.*

As Ocie slinked by, the man-baby glared at him. He was none other than the President of China. Sissy provided distraction by pinching her nipple so that a drop of milk glistened on it.

❊ ❊ ❊

Out in the parking lot, Ocie walked in a daze past the presidential limo and secret service vehicles. An agent looked at him and said, "Hey, Mario."

He turned and said, "I'm not—"

"Of course you're not Mario," said an old guy stepping forward. "You're Ocie Odie, and I'm Uncle. So tell me, what do you make of this whole thing?"

Ocie Odie struggled to put it into words. He had been awakened, he had been transformed, he had become a man, he had been crushed. He had seen his own forgotten childhood, and how he had been shaped, molded, ever since then. His perceptions of the Double D had altered many times, milestones of his metamorphosis. He had been a knight, a horse, a minotaur, and a fool. Then this final revelation, with milky dreams from Europe, America, and China, wherein three world leaders indulged themselves in infantile idiocy. High is low, and low is high. It all crystallized at once, and he blurted out,

"The world is ruled by boobs!"

YOUR LIFE
IS MINE

My hands were around your pale throat, choking you. You clawed at my hands, trying to break my grip, but then you reached for my eyes with your long nails. I saw blood then, but it was not mine—it was yours, spraying from your sliced wrists. Your life essence, flowing into me. Mine.

* * *

Today I go to Alcatraz. Ten days ago I walked in Death Valley. That was the beginning, and today will be the end. I have to write it down.

I've been to Death Valley a few times but I always forget how far across the desert it actually is. On this occasion something had come up in the Mojave, and so I thought I might escape it through a side trip. The drive took a long time, too long, and my agitation was mounting to the screaming point.

I put in a CD and found soothing relief in a song of cool jazz. The drums started off with their primal magic, then the fat bass came in, followed by the crisp stylings of the electric guitar. The chanteuse began singing in Japanese, sending forth a seductive river of darkness with ghostly back up whispers:

> *Deep inside your heart*
> *Sleep sleepy memories*
> *But now that door's about to open.*
>
> *Open your heart and open your eyes*
> *Then pass through the tunnels that appear*
> *Images glide into view and your breath begins to*
quicken.

The saxophone ripped out a wailing solo, gliding, then howling, followed by a drum solo. At last aching last, the woman's voice came back:

> *Sweet visions, sweet visions, that make you hold*
> *your head and sway.*
> *Up it comes, up it comes, the feelings flood as your*
> *heart is pounding away.*

❋ ❋ ❋

When I finally arrived at Death Valley it was too late in the day for any hiking, so I went straight to the luxury hotel. The design and the decor of the place was a romanticized Spanish California, yet inside it felt more like a European resort. (No doubt you know such details better than I, with all your years spent over there.) After visiting my room I went to the garden and found an oasis so steeply terraced that it reminded me of something from Hong Kong—a Tiger Balm garden translated from the tropical to the arid. And that's what I needed, some kind of balm.

I couldn't find any peace, so I went back to my room, changed into swimming trunks, and went to the pool. I swam a few laps, then reclined in a lounge chair and took in the magnificent view, with mountain ranges rising in every direction like the sides of a vast bowl.

But then it bore down upon me, and I felt trapped. There were tunnels around me, dark passages riddling the hotel like holes in a block of Swiss cheese. Back in my room I threw my clothes back on and set out in the opposite direction, into the desert on foot.

After trudging along for a while, I looked back. The hotel seemed strangely familiar from this angle, giving me a sense of deja vu. Watching it, I walked around some more until it was just right. But what was it from?

I made a square frame with my fingers, and there it was—an album cover. I was holding an album in my hands, a copy of "Hotel California." When I lowered it I found myself in a record store, a Wherehouse Records on the west side of Los Angeles, and there you were, stocking LPs.

The pain in my chest was staggering. Yes, there were visions racing through my head, but they were not sweet. I dropped the record and stumbled toward you. You wore short sleeves, and I had to see more. Your hair was black, blonde roots showing, but your arms, your arms were free of tracks and cuts.

Feeling the gaze of this old weirdo, you turned and said, "Can I help you find something?"

You didn't recognize me. I nearly choked on my bile. I had saved your life, and gone through grief for it. You had been selfish, you were selfish, and you would be selfish. I had saved your life, and when I was later in need you refused to lift a finger to help me.

My divorced parents had died a few years apart, two heavy blows for anyone in his twenties, yet all you could say over the long-distance lines was, "Don't be bitter or sad, because it's really a waste of time." Brave words from an ex-junkie; gruff advice from a twice-failed suicide.

Perhaps you tell yourself that I didn't really save you, that I only tried. Maybe, but if I had "failed," as that presupposes, then you would be dead. Since you are not dead, then I did not fail, and your life belongs to me.

That has meaning in the Orient.

I went for the door, wondering if my old car would be there in the parking lot, and I resolved to take a bus if it wasn't. I'd see my mom again, and I'd explain why I couldn't trade your life for her terminal illness. But when I left the Wherehouse, I walked back out into the desert.

I did not know I was going to take back your life, but I now had that goal. A goal I will complete today.

See you soon.

*   *   *

Despite my bold words, I failed. Things have become complicated. I may have to quit.

I had never been to Alcatraz before—have you? The park rangers don't give tours any more, they give visitors pre-recorded lectures to listen to as they go along at their own pace. I took the Japanese language version, just to keep in practice. I thought it might trigger something, but it didn't. So then I listened to the jazz song from before, and still nothing happened.

I was over in D Block, containing the cells for the worst prisoners, when I tried another song by a different band. It was hot jazz, and the female vocalist presented a clash of opposites, mixing perfect English with bar-girl Japanese. Purring at times and snarling at others, she told a story about a mysterious woman of death and destruction. *If you know her, you're already killed in a second . . . But you know her—you spontaneously discharge like that . . . Now the unmasking as the sign is peeled away —don't cry out . . . Don't you know her? An extreme investigation into you.*

And that was it. I walked into the Strip Cell, a solitary confinement cell with no light and no furnishings. When I closed the heavy door the room was pitch black. The smell of hairspray brought it back—how we'd drift apart and fall together, each time more violently than the last, until I couldn't take it any more. So tell me how it happened, because I don't seem to know. There was always something unsaid, but we had different ideas of what it was.

I was crawling around in the dark, looking for a shirt button or something I'd lost, and the door opened—a small half-door, a hatch. I crawled through it and emerged in the eye socket of Skull Rock. I was in Southern California, in the hills above the town where you were born and raised, a town I lived in for just a few years. To the south lay Santa Monica, with its long pier and wide beach. To the west, beyond the rolling hills and the cliffs of the palisades, I saw the blue Pacific under sunny skies.

"Where'd you go?" you asked, down there on the ground, your hair a garish orange. "I thought you were going to be my spirit guide and it's starting, I think. No, I'm sure. I'm definitely flying."

I clambered down the rock face until I stood before you. I was breathing heavily from the effort, and when you looked at me, you burst out laughing. "Whoa, your face is melting! Ha-ha, like acid."

"If it is too disturbing, don't look." I turned my eyes to the sea, trying to judge the season.

"No, it is kind of cool, like maybe the way you'll look when you're old."

"How do you feel, right now?"

"This is amazing! And so cheap—dirt cheap compared to junk."

"The idea was to try something more life-affirming." I put my hands on your shoulders, close to your neck. Your eyes were so wide and black, as trusting as a puppy. It made me feel sick—I couldn't do it at that point. I closed my eyes and let go. It was dark and I curled up until I was sitting on something soft.

We were at the revival house, the Nuart Theatre, and you leaned over to say, "It's starting now, it's kicking in—I can tell because your face is melting again."

"Is the show tonight *Bad Timing*? Sometimes I think—"

"No, don't try those mind games," you said. "I'm the one who's tripping, not you. And here we are, just like my brother and his friends, dropping acid and watching European head cartoons."

Bad Timing, that was one of your favorite films. The nice guy and the messed-up woman who leads him down a dark path of destruction.

"I have," I said, "this theory that men are attracted by visual arts, which is why pornography exists in film and photos. Women are attracted by song."

"So wait, that makes us twisted, right? Because I sell music and you sell videos."

No, that wasn't it. It was like we were speaking different languages. Perhaps that was always the truth.

"I went west, to the Far East," I said. "You went east, to Italy, cradle of the West."

"Which one of us is tripping?"

I couldn't exactly strangle you in a half-filled cinema. I nodded off, and woke to the white noise of a TV on a dead channel. But it wasn't that, it was the ocean—we were at your parents' beach house, all the way up at county line.

"How many times is this now?" I asked.

"Who's counting?"

"I can't believe it," I said, discouraged at the number and the frequency. Appalled.

"Hey, make a fire in the fireplace for me," you said. "I want a fire."

The fireplace was a metal thing in the corner with a flue going up through the ceiling.

"Later," I said. "Let's go walk on the beach."

"Okay."

There were a couple of night fishermen out. You were laughing at everything at that point. We kept walking into the dark and after a while I made my move.

My hands were around your throat, choking you. Your face turned into someone else's. I yelled and let go.

"What is it?" you asked. "What happened?"

"I saw—your face . . ."

"What did you see?"

"My old girlfriend. She was murdered—strangled. Will be."

"'Wilby'? Was that her name?"

"No," I said, "that's not her name."

"Well, never mind her, let's just try again. Come on, I want you to."

"No."

You took my hands and said, "Oh, so cold. You're trembling! Don't be scared."

You put my hands around your neck, holding them in place.

"Go ahead," you said.

"No," I said, confused at how my plan had been wrong, and ashamed by this strange reversal.

"Come on, do it!"

I pulled my hands away with scratches from your nails.

"You worm," you said. You slapped my face so that my left ear was ringing. I felt shame for my impotence, but I was finally free to speak the unsaid: "When you tried it again, I got the call from your sister."

Just saying it took my wind, bringing back the awful, falling stomach feeling of that moment. I felt dizzy. I closed my eyes for a moment and lowered myself toward the sand, only to meet a chair halfway down.

We were at a table in the psych ward, the bandages on your arms again.

I stood up in the Nuart Theatre.

"I'm going to get something," I said. "You want anything?"

"Red vines."

I made my way to the aisle, trying to see a pattern in the shifting scenes. You seemed to be on heavy drugs each time—even at the hospital. Maybe that was it. I had managed to move back in the sequence, which seemed good. Was the Nuart my heart? Maybe I could control it.

But then I saw an old girlfriend with blonde corkscrew hair sitting with my younger self. It hit me like a punch in the gut, and I staggered on with my eyes averted. I felt sick, but every film I'd ever seen there flickered through my mind—Nicholas Roeg, Kurosawa, David Lynch, Andy Warhol, John Waters, and all the others.

By the time I reached the lobby I had regained my *wa*. There was a song playing that was vaguely familiar, but the voice was different, so I figured it to be a cover.

The lobby was empty except for the middle-aged woman behind the snack counter. She was the same ex-girlfriend I'd just glimpsed in the rows as a teen.

"Hey, long time," she said.

"That's funny, I thought I just saw you inside."

"Sure," she said, nodding.

I noticed a CD case displayed on top of the glass counter. It had her picture on it.

"You didn't have that in the '80s," I said. "You couldn't even play the guitar until I taught you."

"We're not in the '80s."

"Where—?" I started, then backtracked. "Okay, okay. We're not in the '80s, fine. Help me out—how are you here? So far I've seen a ghost and a person on drugs—you aren't dead, are you?"

"No, I sent you a copy of my CD," she said. "You'll be getting it soon."

Then the song hit me. It was her voice but the backup voice was not mine. I picked up the CD case and saw her husband and their two young kids, a boy and a girl. It cut me like a knife. I bit back the mean remarks that flooded my mouth.

"I once knew a girl who slashed her wrists," I said, failing to keep my voice steady. "I tried to help her. She tried it again."

"I know," she said. "I remember. You wrote some songs—"

"She's in there now," I said. "I'm trying to get back something I lost."

"It seems bad," she said, shaking her head.

"Are you running interference for her? Is that it?"

"No, it's not." She cocked her head to the side and asked, "So, what did you lose? What's going on with you, really?"

When she put it like that, I sighed, then I laughed at my sigh. "It's just a mid-life crisis, I guess. A point where everything seems 'over.' My life seems over, but worse—like I never even started. I'm now older than my mom was when she died, and in a few years I'll be as old as my biological father when he died."

"I remember your mom's funeral," she said, softly.

"That's right, you were there. Thank you for that kindness, flying down. In fact, I was at your place when my ex-stepsister left a message on my machine. So then I rushed out, got the first flight, and arrived too late."

"It was very sad," she said.

"And somewhere around in there, after I got back, I called suicide girl, who was at school in Illinois, I think? How did I get her phone number? Must've been through her sister. Anyway, I called her up and she just gave me the big brush off."

She nodded to the theater door and said, "Maybe you should just get back up on that pony."

In anger I turned and headed for the street door. Maybe she was wrong—maybe my car would be in the parking lot, and if not I'd take a bus.

I stepped out in Alcatraz.

Back when I was trying to save your life, when I walked into your house the first time after your first time, I felt like there was something transmitted from your parents to me. They were silently begging me to save you, and without a word I said I would. But I saw it then as a teen —that you were in a bad state; you were hanging out with junkies and prostitutes and punk rockers. Now I see it as an adult. You had everything that I ever wanted—a mother, a father, a brother, a sister—and you were trying to destroy them all by killing yourself.

How could you?

The whole thing makes me sick.

* * *

The end has come, several months later in Yosemite.

I was driving too fast at night and I hit a bear. When I got out of the car I found it wasn't a bear, it was a Native American medicine man.

I got him into the car and drove, looking for an emergency room. He was delirious, saying he was Sicilian, that all the best Indians are Sicilian, and that the white man had turned Yosemite Valley into a German Black Forest for his Aryan fantasies.

The road twisted and turned like it was in a canyon. That seemed strange to me until we emerged at the edge of Santa Monica. Now at least I knew where the hospital was—on the same street as the Nuart Theatre.

When we got to the hospital I asked him how he was and he said, "Better, thanks."

I said, "I should take you inside."

He said, "We are here for you, not me. But don't worry, I'll go with you."

I knew then that my grandmother was dying on one floor and you were in the psych ward on another floor.

We left the car, went into the hospital, and got into the elevator. I pushed the button for the psych ward. I worried that there would be no visiting hours at night, but when the doors opened, the windows of the place were lit by sunshine.

We walked into the day room. At first you had that wounded look, but when you saw I wasn't alone, you glared.

The people around us were mental patients. Some were pacing, some were rocking in place, and a few were turning their faces left to right as if reading a giant page. We spoke of trivial things— they wouldn't let you have your Walkman; there was no unabridged English translation of *The Count of Monte Cristo.* You and I talked, and with each sentence I got further away, unable to speak more than the old trivia that spooled out of our mouths like ticker tape.

Then we left you there. My heart was heavy. I had accomplished nothing.

In the elevator he said, "What now?"

I admitted I didn't know.

"Want to go to the beach? A walk along the pier might do you some good."

I shook my head.

"Hey, let's go see a movie."

I gave in on that one. Outside it was night again. We got into the car and I drove two miles up to the Nuart Theatre. The marquee said "YOUR LIFE IS MINE." We bought tickets and went inside. In the lobby he said, "I'll wait for you here. Get some popcorn, and something for her, then go in."

I did what he said. The movie had already started. The theater was empty except for you sitting alone at dead center. I made my way down to you. The film was set at some sort of mental institution. The patients were shuffling like zombies or nodding their heads to invisible music.

I sat next to you and handed over the red vines.

You said thanks, and gestured at the screen weakly, saying, "This . . . I don't know. Like a Warhol film? Slow."

In the movie two guys entered the scene and made contact with a female patient. They sat at the table and started talking.

I turned to you and said we could go. One of the mental patients looked straight into the camera at that moment.

"No," you said. "It can't last forever."

The young woman was complaining that they

had confiscated her Walkman.

I turned to you and said, "Hey, my mom once told me this little thing, almost like a parable—this guy has a bad day at work, so when he comes home he gives the kid a hard time; the kid kicks the cat; the cat goes outside and kills a mouse. That's where it ends, the dead mouse."

You said, "Huh."

Having said it, I found I didn't know why I had said it. I'm not sure exactly what the parable meant. I don't like the idea of a feeling being transmitted down a "kicking order" to the point where it grounds out in a death, but maybe sometimes things are really like that.

I don't know why you tried the first time; I don't know why you tried the second time. There might be some solid answer, or it might just be typical teenage anxiety over the future. I tried to help. In some hidden corner of my mind I thought that you had taken from me some essence, that you had taken some part of me, something of me was incorporated into you.

I said, "At the twenty-year class reunion, people said, 'Wow, you've changed—you used to be so happy.'"

"I'm surprised you went."

"So am I. You weren't there, you were still in Italy."

You sprouted up into a giant monstrosity with waving tentacles. Your eyes the size of dinner plates shone with a junkie's red glaze. A trail of slime dripped from your slack mouth. You took me up in a tentacle, squeezing me like a doll.

I saw that I was wrong—there was no trace of me in you. Instead I had passed through you like something you had eaten.

We were at the center of a red web that filled the theater. You were a spider demon, a personification of feminine destruction. The people in the movie were watching us, quitting their lines for the real show.

You held me higher, above your upturned face, and squeezed harder, your demented features given animation by demonic glee. I struggled, pounding my fists against your tentacle, trying to break your grip, but I also wondered if there was any point—you had eaten me before, so did it matter if you ate me again?

You squeezed harder and I felt something coming up my throat. I lifted my hands to my mouth just as I vomited, and caught something emerging from me. I suddenly saw that I had something of yours—that our positions were opposite of what I had thought. In my hands I held your mewling darkness, your suicidal selfishness. I had carried it away from you and so you lived, but I still carried it, forgotten, these decades later. A disease.

You hesitated then, surprised. You were shrinking, or I was growing. I jammed my left hand into your mouth to block it open, and then I thrust my other fist with the inky thing past your slavering lips, between your shark teeth, through your fetid mouth, and down your throat. There was a blast, and you were just a confused middle-aged academic.

I came to in Yosemite. The bear was dead; the car was smashed; the CD was cracked.

I don't know how it seemed to you, but I am free of it now. Maybe your accomplishments suddenly seem hollow. Maybe you are yearning again for the instant satisfaction of heroin. Maybe it is just a mid-life crisis.

I walk through this vale of disappointment, flanked by shadowy figures that call me Daddy, but they don't count.

THE DONKEY'S TALE

O kay, to start off, my real name is Donkey O'Tay. You can call me Don.

Yeah, I hate that other nickname, but looking back on the whole thing, those names they gave us are pretty dodgy—some of us guys even got girly names. So I guess I was lucky, compared to that.

My main complaint was that I was forced into always being the responsible one, like I was the only adult in the group, or worse, like I was the bloody parent of these tumbling little party animals. Things were pretty wild at times, always on the verge of spinning completely out of control. I'd try to do something constructive like, and they'd come roaring in and smash it all up. There were all sorts of necessary cover-ups, like when Ed suddenly starts wearing a shirt, new "fashion" thing, but in reality it is to hide a tattoo or some pierced nipples he'd picked up on holiday with the Weasels in the Wild Wood.

Yeah, like rock stars before there was rock stars. That's a good one.

Now, I understand the need in light comedy for a straight man, but still. I mean, can you imagine? Twenty-four hours a day, seven days a week. It's pretty blasted exhausting, and I needed a holiday of my own. And not just the usual Wild Wood weekend.

No, we never hoofed it all the way to the Wild Wood. That's seventy or eighty miles! See, Ed had this deal with the station masters so's we could travel *in-cog-hidden,* as he liked to say. We'd go to the train station at Hartfield and get into this big trunk with the label "Mr. Saunders, to Pangbourne" on it. Shipped as freight, that's right, and before long, we'd be out there by Toad Hall.

It's a different crowd, but it's pretty much the same as the home field. Still, there was this one salty old rat they called The Wayfarer. He had really been places. Abroad, overseas, and like that. I met him a few times with the Weasels. At some point or the other he told me about this far off place, and it sounded perfect for me. So, very quiet like, I made plans, booked passage, and all that.

Well, they caught wind of it, sure enough. No secrets possible around there. And they felt kind of bad—not 'cause they had been running me ragged, mind you! Oh no! Only that I was being so antisocial and "selfish" as to want to go off alone for a while.

Next thing you know they was all piling on to go with, saying, "Come on, Don! It'll be fun! This time will be different—you're the leader."

I thought, "Yeah, right. I'll be cleaning up after you guys, as usual, as well as serving as the butt of jokes, the target of 'accidents.'" But I really wanted to go to the place, having heard so many great things about it, and I even thought that they might not like it much at all, which would serve them right—for once they could be sad and glum while I had the time of my life!

So yeah, a bit of revenge-seeking on my part. "Passive aggressive," is it?

We got on the boat, or ship, or what have you. It was all kind of shady so I won't say more about that. The main point is that the vessel in question wasn't stopping at the resort island, it was just going by it. To get from ship to shore we used the umbrella-boat trick for the first time. Before too long, the four of us—donkey, tiger, bear, and pig—were standing on the beautiful beach at Pleasure Island.

What? Don't look at me like that. It makes sense, don't it? Perfect sense. At the time.

We had the whole place to ourselves, at first. It was kind of the off-season, I guess. My friends fed their carnal appetites with more than their usual gusto, if such can be imagined, while I entered a series of self-guided workshops: in the house building section I studied architecture and practiced carpentry; in the museum I studied the masters and tried my hand at art. I felt like Michelangelo, like I was turning into a real renaissance donkey. It was paradise, and in the back of my mind I wondered if we would ever go back home to Chris.

Then the regular boat came and unloaded a horde of boys. They were not at all like Chris, not one of them. I don't know if they were Americans or just Italians, but everything went to hell when they stormed through the place. Instead of building forts or tree houses they were breaking every house and cottage. Instead of admiring art, or creating it, they were destroying any art they found.

"Time to leave," is what I said to myself, and I got over to the donkey corral lickety-split, figuring that I'd be safe there. Sure, the donkeys I found were all sad and crying, but that's a donkey's lot, in'it? And I thought they was glum over the prospects of leaving the island.

That's when I found out how wrong I'd been. You can see it, I'm sure. I'd taken the place to be for donkey recreation, not donkey creation.

I felt duped by my own dreams, but I still figured we four were all safe enough. "Thank God Chris didn't come," is what I said. Then Tig came bounding over in a state of high botheration.

"Ed and Pig in trouble!" he said. "Bad boys doing terrible things!"

"Like what?" I asked, slow to stir.

"Kicking the stuffing out!"

That's all I needed to hear. I know for you folks that phrase is just an expression, but for us it is very real, and very, very bad.

So I tore back to town like a thoroughbred or something. You won't believe it, because normally Tig is the fastest of us, but at a couple of points he was riding on my back 'cause he couldn't keep up.

The place he drove me to was a cozy little thatch-roof cottage. Right off I could see that Ed and Pig had been laying in supplies for a tea party, the sort of thing they do. Now the place was a terrible mess, and my poor friends were being beaten.

"Hey you!" I yelled from the doorway, Tig beside me. I meant to tell them the truth, about how they was being turned into donkeys. In the sudden silence, I said, "You're all . . ." But all their eyes were on me, and those eyes were so bad, so very, very bad, that I lost my voice.

Tig saved us. "Let's party!" he shouted, bouncing up and down like a pogo. "Party time!"

But then he said the worst thing. Much worse than if I had tried to explain about their coming doom of donkey-hood. Yet to him, it was the best thing, the happiest thing in all the world.

"Birthday Party!"

You don't get it? I'm a donkey, standing in the doorway, and somebody shouts, "Birthday Party"? Maybe they were Americans after all, in which case

I should be grateful they weren't Mexicans.

You still don't get it? All right, look . . . they tore off my tail and chased me around, trying to pin it back on me.

Sure there was pain and humiliation in that, but at the time I was too busy for such, seeing as how I was tearing around in a circle. I wouldn't be surprised if I left tracks on the walls, you know it? Braying my head off whenever the pin would stick me. It was awful.

After a few laps I noticed that my friends had vanished. "Poor me," I thought to myself, and I'd have sat down and died right there iffin it warn't so very painful.

A dozen more laps and I was running out of steam. I knew the end was coming, but I just kept kicking. They were closing in for the kill, when suddenly a frightened confusion came across us all in the form of pungent smoke.

"Now's the time to blow out the candles!" said Ed's voice from the cold fireplace, because he was shouting down the chimney from the roof.

The thatch roof was on fire!

The boys piled out the door. I found my tattered tail on the floor, snatched it up, and I was right behind them. While the boys were distracted by the spectacle of a house fire, I rejoined my friends and we ran away to safety.

When we got to the beach, my feelings were fighting with each other. On the one hoof I was happy, on the other hoof I was alarmed.

"Ed!" I said.

"You saved us, Don," he said. "We couldn't leave you behind."

"I appreciate that, and thank you for saving me," I said slowly. "But I worry . . . you torched the house, that's arse-on!"

They busted up at that, what you call an accidental pun. They were rolling on the sand, laughing their heads nearly off. And I had to laugh, too.

"Look, Don, we'll make a promise," said Ed, wiping a tear from his eye. "What happens in Pleasure Island, stays in Pleasure Island. All right?"

We shook on it.

After all that, we had a devil of a time getting back home. And then we had to cook up some cock and bull story about my tail. It was a cover story for me this time. But after such an adventure abroad it was truly great to be back.

STORIES TO
THE FUTURE

R ust belt city. Population decline. Conurbation as organism; coral, perhaps. The end of another soul-crushing office day. No future.

Alone at the bus stop, a twenty-two year old office worker named Philip checked his mobile phone. He looked up at a thunderous sound down the block to discover a stagecoach racing straight at him.

He jumped out of the way, flattening himself against the building. The juggernaut roared past like an express train of muscle and wood.

There was something squishy about the phone in his hand. The device had become a lump of rotting hamburger meat adorned with a human ear and lips. He dropped it in disgust, gagging with revulsion.

Sweat ran down his face and neck as he gaped at the weathered brick beside him. The office building was no longer the edifice of chrome and glass he had left a few minutes before. But the riveting detail was a hanged man, an executed criminal left on public display.

He heard inarticulate whimpering sounds nearby, then discovered he was making them.

Philip found himself on a street that looked like a tourist attraction, some sort of medieval reconstruction. The road was narrow, the buildings were shoulder to shoulder but only a few stories high. There were towers off in the distance. The scent of rotting rubbish, human waste, and horse sweat filled the air. His rust belt city was gone.

An eerie warbling resounded in the distance. Staring in that direction, he could just make out a giant brazen idol with a bullhead.

"Faithful come to Melech," sang a voice, distorted as if produced by an electric amplifier or bullhorn. "Lay down all thought, surrender to Lord Melech."

Panicking, Philip ran into the building he had sheltered against. Inside there was a lift with its car doors open. He rushed in and jabbed the highest button, but when the doors closed the lift dropped instead of rising.

It seemed to be an express, and it plunged for a long time.

Finally the car slowed, then stopped. The floor

indicator read "CM." The doors opened upon a sunny swampland crossed by many low hedges. Philip pushed the highest button again, but nothing happened.

He stepped out with caution, keeping close. He emerged from the trunk of a petrified tree. What Philip had taken to be a hedge he now saw as some form of land coral studded with fossils of artifacts from the technological world, such things as eyeglasses, bicycles, TVs, home computers.

The lift doors shuddered so he jumped back in. His ears popped on the way up. The indicator light flashed "L" then up a few more before slowing for the end at "M."

Philip stepped out of the lift. The floor, presumably termed a mezzanine, was unfamiliar, and the windows offered a bird's-eye view of a strange city.

He slumped against the wall.

Why did I go inside the building? he wondered. *Why go up? Trying to find my office, trying to find someplace normal. What is happening to me—am I going mad?*

Perhaps it is the stress of working too hard during the day, and playing too hard at night. That sounds good—plausible at least. Take it easy, mate—life kills. You need rest. Maybe I can find a place to take a quick nap, then everything will be A-OK.

Philip leaned on the window, looking out on the city. The bull-headed idol was still there, near the horizon, but the streets had cars rather than stagecoaches. The cars were old-fashioned, though, very antique. The transition from carriage to horseless-carriage had him wondering if he had moved through time by going up in the building.

There was no lift going up from this floor, but he found an escalator and went up three levels. From the windows at this height the automobiles were hard to see in detail, but in the air above the city moved a zeppelin with cuneiform markings.

The banks of escalators ended at this story, but Philip located a carpeted stair and ran up a few flights in the fevered belief he could climb back to the future in this way. The stairs ran out at the top of the building, at what appeared to be an abandoned construction site for a story not yet begun. There was a self-standing ladder, though, and having gone this far he endeavored to take the last step. He climbed up the rickety rotting thing and at the top, being at the elevation of the next floor, the cityscape looked more modern than it had at the foot.

The brazen idol in the distance now towered higher still. In fact, it was the highest structure in sight.

Overwhelmed, Philip climbed down off the ladder. He lay down against the wall, closed his eyes, and was fast asleep.

* * *

He awoke with a feeling of immediate danger.

Moonlit now, the setting was otherwise the same as before. He started. A man in the shadows watched him.

"You looked so peaceful," said the man.

"Sorry," said Philip as he got to his feet, "I felt wiped out, so I took a nap. I didn't mean to trespass."

"Don't worry, I'm a stranger here myself."

"So the building isn't locked for the night?"

"I wouldn't know," said the man. "I haven't been inside."

Philip did a double take but refrained from comment, instead saying, "Well, I guess I'll find out." He tried the door and it opened. "So far, so good."

"Mind if I go with?" said the other.

"Not at all," said Philip, skin crawling.

They went down several flights. The stranger was a pasty fellow dressed in black. At each floor Philip looked around for a toilet. Finally he spotted a Gents and went to it.

"I'll just duck in here," he said over his shoulder.

"Let me go with you," said the stranger.

"No," Philip said with a shudder of revulsion.

"But—"

"I'll just be a minute."

Philip went in alone, relieved to be getting away from the creep.

The facilities were decidedly old fashioned, perhaps mid-twentieth century, yet perfectly adequate. As Philip washed his hands he looked around, wondering if he would go out the window to avoid the creep.

There were two windows, in fact, and between them a door as if for a balcony or fire escape. Curious, he opened it and found a dark room, cramped and crowded with discarded office furniture, a room where there could not be a room.

Philip looked through the window again and saw a view of the city uninterrupted by the walls of the room beyond the door.

"Hello," said a man's voice from the darkness. "I didn't realize there was another door. That makes sense. Ingenious."

"Hello?" said Philip, peering into the storage room.

"I'm Eric," said a shape. "You must be my contact. May I come out?"

"Sure, yes," said Philip. "Please do." He stepped aside and made a sweeping gesture of welcome.

A middle-aged man appeared, wearing the blue overalls of an auto mechanic or factory worker.

"Do you have a lot of experience with this sort of thing?" Eric asked. His face was gaunt, his hollow cheeks marked by stubble. "Obviously I have none."

Philip shut the door and asked, "What 'sort of thing'?"

Eric's eyes widened in fear. He swallowed.

"I want to get out," he said, looking down at his hard-worn shoes. "Out of the country. Defect."

"Re—ally," said Philip, bewildered.

"Yes, absolutely."

"Why?"

"Someone wants my job," said Eric, glancing around with anxiety. "Someone in this building. My life is in danger. I put myself in your hands—"

The restroom door banged open as the creep barged in with, "What's all this, then?"

Eric panicked, went for the odd door, but Philip held it shut.

"Don't worry," said Philip, "he's not after you, he's after me. But while we're here, look out that window."

"Seemed like you were taking an awful long time," said the creep, "and then I heard voices of a most intimate nature."

"Hey," said Eric, looking out the window. "That's weird."

"Isn't it?" said Philip. He laughed with nervous relief. "You don't know how good it makes me feel to hear you say that!"

"Let me join in," said the sullen creep.

"All right. Look out the window."

"What am I looking for?"

"Now look inside this door."

"Whoa. That's—that's . . . impossible."

"I thought I was going mad."

"Madness likes company," said the creep.

"Really? I thought it was the opposite."

They left the lavatory. Philip led them down the hall, Eric speaking to him in undertone:

"Sorry about that back there. I'm no Joe Soap, really—I just saw his black clothing and assumed he was Inner Party."

They passed the lift, prompting Eric to ask why they did not take it. Philip told him his concern with express elevators in the building, and as they went down many flights of stairs he told them of his adventure.

On a floor between the mezzanine and the lobby they heard a distant yelling.

They hurried, following the sound to find an open window framing a man outside, hunched over, surrounded by smoke and flames.

"Help!" cried the man, his face ugly as a beast. "My arm—my arm!"

The man's arm was caught in some sort of vice trap along the lower edge of the window that pinned him in place. Philip rushed over and struggled to release the trap. Glancing out he saw the man was in a burning tree. Eric helped Philip pry at the trap, and then the bar pressing the arm to the sill opened. The man, now freed, leaped through the open window, his naked back smoldering.

"I thank you all!" he said, panting on hands and knees. "I beg you, let them take me not."

"Who's after you?" asked Philip.

"The ones who hunt," said the man.

"Hunters?"

"The monster hunt," said the fellow, and when he looked up, Philip could see his point: the man's head was not human, it was more akin to that of an orangutan. Most disturbing were his eyes, having no whites to them, being as fully colored as an ape's.

Philip and Eric recoiled from him.

"Be not afraid," said the man-ape. "I mean no harm for you. Just leave, and know forever more my debt."

The heat blazing through the window was rising.

"Your arm," said Philip. "Is it broken?"

"It might be so," admitted the man-ape, but then he shook his head. "No, fine it is. With Luck, headfirst I came not in this way! Forsooth I would have met my maker here."

He got up and they all took a few steps away from the heat.

"It's a burglar trap," said the creep. "Are you a thief?"

"No," said the man-ape with a big square-tooth grin that seemed small above that massive chin. "Forsooth, I am astony to find a building here. In woods I was long running, near forspent. So climb a tree I did, to hide in cockshut dusk. Among the boughs I spied a glassy pane."

"So there wasn't a building there before?" asked Philip.

"Of buildings there were none. 'Twas dusk, yet not so black as that. But hark, my eyes were wrong, for here I am."

The man-ape gave his name as Charles

Piltdown. Philip invited him to join them in going downstairs and then outside, if they might find a door unlocked.

"What then?" queried Charles. "If I may ask."

"I want to go see that giant idol—"

"Lord Melech, do you mean?"

"Yes, I've heard that name. Do you know it?"

"Who knows it not?"

"I don't," said Eric.

"Nor do I," said the creep.

"Then again," said Eric, turning to the creep, "I don't recall how you came into this strange tower."

"He implies he flew to the roof," said Philip, drily.

"Like a . . . fairy?

"Like a bat," snapped the creep.

"Oh," said Eric, nodding with mock enthusiasm. "You mean a fruit bat."

"You mean to say," said Charles, "you flew from outside air?"

The creep nodded in superior fashion.

"Are you all outlanders, that Melech you know not?"

Philip told Charles his adventure. The man-ape listened attentively, then asked, "And at the idol, what is it you seek?"

"I hope we can climb up to my level there. All of us. It's a better place."

Charles offered to lead them to Melech, should they be able to leave the building.

The group of four went downstairs, crossed the

lobby, and emerged on the street with the hanged man.

Charles turned to Philip and said, "This place is not the world you call your home?"

"Correct."

"Did someone help you come to here from there?"

"No."

"Then how to here did you contrive to come?"

"I don't know."

"Your hand allow for my examination please?" When Philip agreed, the man-ape held his hand with both of his own, then looked deep into his eyes.

"Ah!" said Charles. "In love you are, I clearly see, young man."

"Ah-ha!" crowed the creep.

"What?!" cried Philip.

Charles released his hand and said, "I now shall lead you all to where you wish."

"But—but this makes no sense!" sputtered Philip as he hurried to catch up.

"'Tis rare that Love make sense in any way."

"But I'm not in love!"

"In truth thou art, my friend from time afar."

"Even if I were, how would that explain anything?"

"In poetry find truth, to whit: You fell."

"'Fell'?"

"Fell hard, or so it would appear to me."

"So, then . . ." Philip looked at the medieval city

around them, the corpse hanging from the gibbet, the rats scurrying in the garbage along the street. "This is love?"

"The feeling, yes, from past unto the end."

"It's not what I imagined," said Philip. "Not at all."

"It never is, if truth be told, my friend."

＊ ＊ ＊

A loud noise of flutes and drums filled the whole area before the idol so the cries of wailing should not reach the ears of the people.

When the flames licked a living child the limbs contracted like a spider on a hot plate, and the open mouth seemed almost to be laughing until the body slipped quietly into the brazier.

＊ ＊ ＊

Philip pushed his way out of the idol complex, the other three behind him. A man stepped into his way, and held Philip's shoulder in a firm grip.

"You turn away from Melech."

"Yes," said Philip. He tried to shrug off the hand.

"In horror and disgust."

"Yes," said Philip, wishing he could scrub the recent images from his mind. "I had no idea."

"Come with me," said the man, releasing his

shoulder. "We have a different way, a better way."

They followed the guide across the city, finally arriving at a small, three-storied building. It seemed unexceptional, but when they were about to enter it, Philip looked up and gasped.

"What?" asked Eric.

"It seems taller here, doesn't it? That seems like a good sign."

The others squinted, scowled.

"Don't you see it?" asked Philip. "It sort of shimmers at the top?"

His companions signified the negative through different grunts and gestures.

Inside the building they followed their guide across a lobby to a lift. Inside the car, the dial showed "L," "M," and "H."

"'Lobby,'" said Philip, "and 'Mezzanine,' but what is 'H'?"

"No," said the guide. "'H' is for 'Head,' 'M' is for 'Middle,' and 'L' is for 'Legs.'"

Charles was startled when the small room began to move. They explained it to him.

On the third floor they exited the car and went down a short hallway. Beyond a big double door they encountered a giant head and shoulders that emerged from a close-fitting hole in the floor. This noggin was over three feet from crown to chin. On its thick neck it towered over seven feet above the floor.

"Hallo!" boomed the head, eyes twinkling. "Come in, come in. I am so glad to meet you fellows

—you came from the haunted tower, did you not? Many people go in, but none come out, whereas you, sir, went in alone and came out with three others. Most extraordinary!"

"How did you know that?" asked Philip.

"Some crows told me. So it is true? Incredible!"

Philip told of his adventure, introducing the others to their host Tom along the way.

When the travelogue was done, Tom the giant said, "I believe we can help each other. You are searching for a way to the hundredth floor, and it is my ambition to grow that tall myself."

"But, surely, that will take time?" said Philip.

"Months, perhaps," said Tom, dismissively. "Less than a year, certainly. So let's buckle down!"

"But is there no place already having one hundred stories?"

"Sadly, there is only Melech—abhorrent, repugnant place! The horror of religious superstition such as that has no place in my vision. Together let us build a stairway to aftertime—a rational place of freedom and justice!"

"That would mean building ninety-seven floors," said Philip. "Whereas, we might complete the haunted building for one tenth of that."

"Alas," said Tom, "'tis a fact that nobody comes out of there. The workers refuse to go, and were they somehow forced, they would not come back.

"As for myself, a project of this magnitude requires an army of workers, and I want you four to be my generals."

The creep spoke up, asking, "May we have a moment to discuss this?"

"Of course! Take five minutes."

Back in the hallway, the creep murmured to Philip, "Let's go along with him here, and I'll try to get the other tower finished."

* * *

They took up lodging at the pondside coach inn. Early on they tried the creep's plan of finishing the haunted tower's construction, but it turned out to be more than a few floors, and too big for them to do alone. In a sour-grapes move, the creep said he might stay in the year 1616 anyway, which was where or "when" they seemed to be at this level, but after disappearing for a few days he reappeared with a black eye and a new drive to escape.

Giant Tom seemed to be right that the four possessed talents useful to the project. Because Philip had the haunted tower access and the hawk-like vision, Tom called him his "haggard." For reasons more obscure he called the creep his bloodhound. Charles was "the mathematic" after his knack for numbers, while Eric was "the cutter" for his ability to slice through Gordian Knots of obfuscation put up by officials, guilds, and guild officials.

On the personal side, Eric gorged on ordinary food like a starving man and put on a lot of weight. He burned his blue overalls in the fireplace as if it meant something, and took to wearing local stuff. As for Charles and Philip, one day at the market they saw a traveling freak show with a man-ape in tow; Charles later told Philip it was Erasmus Piltdown, his grandfather, and he never went out alone again, fearful of being kidnapped.

The first few scores of stories went up so rapidly that Philip thought the tower would be completed much sooner than Tom had said. It was a whirlwind of work, a blurring between labor and rest, during which they saw a few performances of *Richard III* in afternoons at the coach inn.

Then there was a bottleneck, a bind they had to sweat their way through by scavenging techniques from different levels of higher technology. At the haunted tower's lower levels there were fire escapes allowing a team to descend to ground level of different times, but later floors lacking external stairs meant that the creep would fly solo from a window.

During this phase Philip came by stages to discover the hidden history of the haunted edifice. He found it had been alive, like the Tom tower; but somehow it had been murdered.

When they cleared the bottleneck, the Tom tower surged a growth spurt of a few dozen decks before hitting the next snag. Through tears of frustration the team banged out solutions, often falling asleep during performances of Hamlet.

From different stories of the haunted tower, Philip could see the Tom growing over time, and

Melech shrinking. After more than a year, the goal was almost within grasp. At this moment Philip found an executive suite in the haunted tower, and in searching the place he found a box with a written message attached, which read:

To My Vindicator,

Thou art mine own arm of vengeance from beyond the grave. O Horus, O Hamlet, heed my call!

Within this box find the Seed of Destruction. Introduce it to the Usurper's feeding floor. You will have time enough to leave, but not much more.

Philip opened the box to find only a small dark sphere, looking something like a dull black pearl. When he picked it up he was surprised to discover it to be incredibly heavy for such a small thing, heavier than lead.

With completion so near, Tom began to openly brag about how he had killed the haunted tower years before, thereby solving that mystery.

Philip considered the vengeance device. He knew that Tom's feeding floor was in the basement, his nutrition system being more like that of a tree in this regard. On the day when the hundredth floor was finished enough for their purpose, Philip led his three companions on a quiet, unannounced tour of the basement.

It was a vast bio-mass conversion plant, turning organic waste into energy. Then Charles, snooping around, found a hatch leading down, and they discovered the sub-basement.

Catacombs. Tunnels. Like a nest of ants, but

instead of nurseries and food storage rooms they found cavities of a more sinister nature. Suicide closets. Euthanasia suites. Murder cult sacrificial altars. Torture chambers. Duty To Die stations.

From each flowed a crimson creek, which merged together into a river of blood. This was the feeding floor. It was worse than Melech, and on a scale that defied comprehension.

The four visitors were appalled, even the creep, who called it "pornographic."

Philip took out the super-heavy seed of destruction and threw it out into the river. There was an ominous little rumble as they hurried away.

In the lobby they got onto the express lift on the way to their reward at the hundredth floor.

They shared nervous grins as they shot past the fifty mark. They gave a little cheer as they cleared floor sixty. But then at sixty-six the lights went out and the car halted.

Using their combined strength the four pried open the door and climbed out. They ran up the moving escalators, the creep far in front. When the building suddenly swayed, a ceiling pole dropped like a lance, impaling the fast-moving creep.

"No!" shouted Philip.

The three ran on, now Charles in the lead, Eric several lengths behind him, Philip bringing up the rear. The escalators jerked a couple times, then froze, but the men pounded on up them. The glass panes of the wall to the left had shattered, and the wind from a strange age whipped through with an eerie howl. Just as Charles reached a landing, a shudder ran through the building causing a Greek column to fall onto the man-ape, crushing him like a bug.

Numbed, Philip shared an anguished look with Eric.

The remaining two men scrambled over the obstacle and continued racing up the powerless escalators. There were only two stories left to go. Philip's heart felt bursting with the strain, and his legs were heavy, but fear for his life kept him moving, trying to keep up with Eric who remained far in advance.

Another switchback and they were again running next to the shattered glass side of the skyscraper. The howling of the wind made cacophonous choir with the groaning of the building. Suddenly a cable swung down to hit Eric. An electric explosion of sparks tossed his smoldering corpse out the window.

Philip's life flashed before him but he managed to run past the cable.

Then he was on the ninety-ninth floor, and ahead of him was a self-standing ladder leading up. As he ran to the wooden structure, it swayed with the rumbling floor. He leaped onto it and scrambled up the first few steps when a rolling quake hit. He clutched tightly as the ladder walked sideways several inches, threatening to pitch him out into the yawning gulf of space. Struggling to keep balance, Philip surged up its length toward the opening in the floor above.

He threw himself upward and landed his chest on the upper level. He pulled himself up and lay there panting like a lizard on a roof tile, when suddenly the floor fell down to smash the one below, which in turn collapsed. The tower was collapsing like a house of cards. Each fall delivered a heavy blow to Philip's entire body, and the seventh strike beat his consciousness out.

* * *

An angelic voice called to him from above:

"Philip? *Philip!* Hey, are you all right?"

An angel with the voice of an office girl.

He opened his eyes to the pavement at the bus stop. Looking up, he saw her face. His heart sang, and he thought, *Love. Yes, Love!*

From the distance, across the rust belt city, came the faint sound of a call to prayer: "Faithful come to Melech. Lay down all thought, surrender to Lord Melech."

MASTER WU
OF BAMIYAN

I f you weren't so cheap," said his wife, "we would have brought along a spare."

"Yes, my beloved," he murmured, looking over the dead donkey and the one hundred pounds of medicine it could no longer carry.

Dr. Koshyar Ibn-Hashim Attar and his wife, in the process of relocating his pharmaceutical practice from the capital city of Delhi in India to the silk road city of Balkh in Central Asia, had suffered a misfortune of the trail. As a result the young couple found themselves in a forbidding terrain, eight days west of Kabul and two weeks south of Balkh. To go back to Kabul for another donkey would mean leaving their valuables unguarded for sixteen days.

"If you weren't so stingy," she complained bitterly, "we would have hired a dragoman to guide us, and this would not have happened."

"Silence, woman!" he roared. "You'll be the death of me!"

Inspiration came to him at that moment, like lightning to his thunder.

On the ground he arranged the jars and boxes, each containing a type of herb, spice, unguent, mineral, dried plant, or animal product. Together with his wife he built a cairn of stones over it in the style of a grave. Then he prepared a funeral marker of wood, upon which he wrote: "Dr. Koshyar Ibn-Hashim Attar, victim of cholera."

"It is a terrible omen," she said, making a sign with her fingers to ward off the evil eye. "You are tempting the evil spirits. And what makes you think any grave robbers out in this wasteland can read?"

"Well, if one *can* read, that will make him think twice."

They left the cache and continued north on their way to Balkh. After sixteen more days they were greatly relieved to reach the town, even though it was much smaller than they had expected. In fact, it was hardly more than a ghost town, the main presence being a frontier fort of the Mongols. Nevertheless, Koshyar spent a few days settling his wife into their new shop before setting out once again with donkeys and a dragoman this time.

On the fourteenth day, Koshyar spotted his landmark, the distinctive hill crested with eerie rock spires.

"There," he told his guide. "It is across from that hill."

"That be the ruins of a fort, yonder," said the man. "Call it 'Red City.'"

They found the cache at midday. Opening it up, Koshyar cried out. It had been despoiled. Nearly half of the jars and boxes were gone, but in their place was a small strongbox he had never seen before. He opened the box to find five pounds of silver and a scrap of parchment with writing on it.

"'I owe you seven pounds of silver,'" he read aloud. "'Master Wu of Bamiyan.'"

The dragoman grunted at that.

"How extraordinary," said Koshyar. Looking over the remains of his cache, he calculated the value of the missing part. "By Allah, the thief knows his prices. Incredible!"

"Now then," he said, turning to his guide. "Where is this place 'Bamiyan'?"

"That be a ghost town, one day west. Past Red City."

"I thought Balkh was nearly a ghost town."

"Huh."

"Is it much worse than that?"

"All ruins, and ghosts. Bad place."

"You've been there before?"

"No, only heard talk."

"Probably exaggerations, all of it. Let's start now."

"No. We go in there, the sun go down, and we

have to sleep there. Better we go morning time."

"Fair enough," said Koshyar. "Who is this Master Wu? You know him?"

"A Chinaman what sells 'lixers and such," said the dragoman. "I seen him at caravansaries in Kabul, an' Qunduz."

"So he's a real man? Good to know we aren't chasing something . . . otherwise. Why would he be at this ghost town?"

"Don't know. Don't want to know."

"Yes, well, seven pounds of silver is compelling."

* * *

They set out the following morning after prayers. As they passed into the valley below the Red City, Koshyar found himself morbidly fascinated by the view of the ruins. What looked like giant melted candles were the remnants of towers. Men had lived there, and died there. The place was positioned to guard this end of the valley quite well, but now it only served as aeries for the hawks that circled lazily above.

"Did the Mongols destroy it?" he asked.

"Who else," said the dragoman.

The slain were of Koshyar's race, his cousins at least. About a hundred years earlier his forefathers had come boiling out of Ghor to the west, conquering and cleansing in the name of Allah. They had conquered Bamiyan; then, by leaps and bounds they had advanced into India, where Delhi became the capital of their Slave Dynasty. But shortly after this new sultanate was founded, the pagan Mongols had swept from the north, driving through the early frontiers first and then the ancestral homeland, leaving a swath of destruction behind them. Thus, while the colony in India thrived, the original homeland was destroyed.

Finally Koshyar tore his eyes away, only to see a new sight that made him gasp. Across three leagues of valley floor he saw two stone giants standing out from the high cliffs. His mind reeled as he struggled to estimate their size—the smaller statue must be over a hundred feet tall, and the tall one nearly twice that.

He halted and made the warding off gesture with his fingers before he came to his senses. Embarrassed, he looked to the dragoman, afraid to see him jeering, but the man said only, "We go back?"

"No," said Koshyar, stung by the temptation. Thinking of the money, he worked up his courage and said, "We must retrieve what is mine."

* * *

Koshyar struggled to avoid looking at the giants that they were walking toward. For a time he tried to stare at spots on the horizon, at anything that was not the giants, but again and again he found his eyes drawn to them, just like a moth to a candle flame. Frustrated, he tried the opposite, to stare at them so hard that he might bore through them, or at least gain mastery over them.

Now Koshyar saw that the upper face was missing from the larger giant. The evil eyes had been removed, literally. This gave him a thrill, seeing a dent in the terrible tyranny of those frightful effigies.

After some leagues they spotted more ruins, this time on the valley floor, a few miles south and out of their way. Koshyar asked the dragoman about them.

"Must be the real city," said the guide. "What they call 'City of Noise.'"

"'Noise'? It seems so silent."

"From the noise when they was being killed."

Turning back to their track west, Koshyar saw a peasant who had stopped his work in the fields to come up to the path, staring at them in suspicion. When they reached the spot, there were three peasants. The dragoman asked them if their village was Bamiyan. Sullenly, they admitted it was. The guide asked them where Master Wu could be found. One of them pointed to the two giants.

Koshyar and the dragoman walked another league until they came to the land at the feet of the giant statues. The cliff face around the giants was dotted with caves high and low. The only person visible was a wizened Chinese man, who seemingly sat waiting for them. As they walked into conversational range, he stood and said, "Do I have the pleasure of meeting Doctor Koshyar?"

"Yes," said Koshyar. "You are Master Wu?"

"I am, indeed," said the man. "I'm very surprised to see you so soon. I must say, you look remarkably well for a dead man!" Wu beamed at his own joke, but seeing Koshyar frown, Wu switched tack, adopting a scholarly mien. "'Koshyar' is an unusual name," he said, stroking his wispy chin beard. "The only time I have ever encountered it before was in the writings on the legendary Avicenna."

"You've read Avicenna?" said Koshyar, wondering if this was part of the patter the man used to overawe the semi-literate.

"Only in translation, of course. But if my failing memory serves, Koshyar was a physician who taught Avicenna."

"Yes, that's right," said Koshyar, impressed. "Few people know that." He grudgingly admitted to himself that the man was more than a simple charlatan, perhaps a complex one.

"Are you also a physician yourself, like your namesake?"

"Alas, I am only a pharmacist."

"Too bad! I was hoping for a second opinion. In any event, welcome to Bamiyan, former capital of a kingdom that once stretched as far north as Balkh."

"Is that so?" asked Koshyar. "I've just moved to Balkh from Delhi."

"Ah, a brave new tradesman for the Mongol empire. Perhaps the empty houses will fill again. Have you any Shibarghan melons with you? I shouldn't ask, but . . . ."

"No, I do not. What are they?"

"Their fame does not stretch even to Delhi? Why, they are the best melons in the world! They dry them in strips, you see. Wonderful trade item, delicious gifts."

"I shall have to look into that," said Koshyar. "Now then, may we discuss the reason for my visit?"

"I know you want what is due to you, but I must admit that I did not expect you to visit so soon. Allow me to explain my side of things, as we stroll to yonder cave."

"All right."

They began walking, and the dragoman followed with the donkeys.

"Now then," said Master Wu. "There came a day when I found myself in dire need of medicinal supplies, and so I took what silver I had and set out for Kabul. By what seemed to be exceptional good fortune, I found your buried treasure scarce five leagues away! I took what I needed, leaving all my silver and the note."

"Do you make a habit of robbing graves?" asked Koshyar with irritation.

"Ah," said Wu with a sympathetic smile. "Your ruse, while clever, was undone by a few points. First, the dead donkey drew vultures, which caught my attention from miles away. When I investigated the carcass, I found nearby the tracks of a man and a boy or a woman, and those of a few donkeys. As a result, I was slightly suspicious when I saw the grave, and after I had read the marker, I knew."

Koshyar bit his lower lip in vexation over how he had inadvertently left a beacon for his hidden stash. Master Wu continued on.

"Here we are, some weeks later. You have come for your payment, which is right and proper, but I have no silver at this time."

"Then you can start by giving me back the portion you did not pay for."

"Yes, that would be a sensible solution," said Master Wu, "but for the fact that it is already used up."

"All? But that would be enough for many people."

"It is true. I find I am running a sick house." Master Wu paused for a moment. "This is how it came to pass: A holy man from far Cathay came here, to these ruins, as a pilgrimage. Many monks came with him, for he is an abbot, but now they are sick and he is dying."

"What is the disease?"

"Do you know the plague of Justinian?"

"No."

"Ah. Well, their path here was different than yours—coming from Delhi, you came through Kabul?"

"Yes."

"They passed through Charikar, north of Kabul. From thence one can go straight west and arrive here in about a week. Here is my study."

They had reached the mouth of the cave. The dragoman waited outside as the two men of medicine went in. Koshyar found it to be a room carved from the soft stone. There was a chair beside a table with a pile of scrolls, a sleeping platform in one corner, and a doorway into a dark passage beyond.

"When the monks came they were hale and hearty, yet the next morn found them wracked by high fever and swelling blisters. It is also called 'the black death.'"

"Ah, I've heard of that!"

"Listen well, for it is a disease unknown by the ancients, yet it crops up along the silk road where you now live."

"Doesn't it kill everyone it touches?"

"Perhaps it kills two thirds," said Master Wu, stopping beside the table. "The Byzantine Emperor Justinian survived it, hundreds of years ago. His treatment was written down, and I performed what I could for the monks. It ran its course in four days and I'm proud to say that only ten of the thirty-one died."

"Incredible. And all this within four days?"

"Yes, that's right," said Master Wu. He took up one of the scrolls. "That was about two weeks ago. At that time the survivors were very weak. The abbot caught pneumonia. I began treating him for that, but he is not getting better."

"Did you use hydromel?" asked Koshyar as a way of testing him.

"No," said Master Wu, giving him an odd look. "It was oxymel, on the fourth day after purging the bowels, followed by ptisan on the seventh day. But there seems to be a further complication, which is why I ask you to please read this scroll to me."

"Wait a moment," said Koshyar, holding up a hand. Wu had passed the test, but the conversation was wandering off topic. "What about the money you owe me?"

"That is, indeed, a problem," said Master Wu. "This place was stripped bare centuries ago, so I cannot offer you gold leaf scraped off the giants, nor the gems that once adorned them, nor even costly incense previously offered to them. I would not dream of offering you anything that might insult your religious sensibilities. This valley produces no specialty, no musk or melon, that would fill this need. But I cannot send you away empty handed.

"I will give you a device of ancient science, which you will hold as a guarantee in Balkh. Within six months you will have the opportunity to sell it, either to me for seven pounds of silver, or to an alchemist for perhaps more than that."

"Six months?" cried Koshyar. "I'm trying to start a business! Such a wait will cripple me."

"Yes, yes, how thoughtless of me," said Wu,

scratching his cheek. "Make that three months."

"I suppose," said Koshyar.

"Very good. So we have settled that. But now that you are here, could you please help me by reading this one scroll out loud?"

"What is it?"

"It is Hippocrates in Arabic. There are terms I don't understand, and it has bearing on my patient, I believe."

Koshyar felt he was being tricked, somehow. He did not have his silver yet, in fact, he might not ever get it, and he was now being invited to donate free labor. He rapidly thought up a way to turn the tables.

"You will tell me how you treated the monks for this plague?"

"Yes, gladly."

"Please do so now."

"Ah, I see. I will bring a monk for you to examine. Just a moment, please."

Wu went outside and shouted some commands, then gestured for Koshyar to come out.

As they waited for the monk, Master Wu told Koshyar of the treatment. For headache he used rose, lavender, sage, and bay. For nausea he used wormwood, mint, and balm. He used vinegar as a cleansing agent. A plaster of arsenic, lily root, and dried toad applied to the blisters. For blisters in the armpit he used bloodletting from an arm vein, and for blisters in the groin he used bloodletting from a big toe.

Koshyar saw a skeletally thin sallow man in a yellow robe walking towards them, but as the monk came closer, Koshyar saw he had scabs on his bare arms. Master Wu told of the treatment, pointed out details, and acted as translator between the two men.

Satisfied with this lesson, Koshyar opened the scroll at the selected section and began reading aloud. Master Wu listened and interrupted to ask questions about words like *empyema* and *hemithorax*.

When it was over, Master Wu said, "Now then, might we go to examine the abbot, while the wisdom of Hippocrates is fresh in our minds?"

Koshyar acquiesced with ill grace, eager to be away. They went to another cave.

Huasha the abbot was seated in a large wooden tub of warm water, attended by three monks. He rose and bowed to Koshyar as Master Wu introduced them. Abbot Huasha stepped out of the tub, allowed the monks to pat him dry, and then he sat on a chair.

Huasha bowed and said something to Koshyar, which Master Wu translated as, "I am in your hands."

"As the scroll tells us," said Master Wu, "the first thing is to determine in which hemithorax the empyema is located. If you would please, put your ear against his right side, and the monks will shake him."

"All right," said Koshyar. "Let's get this over with."

He listened as they shook the abbot, then he listened at the left side as they shook again. The left side had the sloshing sound of water.

"Excellent," said Master Wu. "Next comes the incision. The bellied scalpel is here."

"Wait, wait, wait!" said Koshyar, holding up his hand. "You want me to do this, now?"

"Yes," said Master Wu. "He will die soon if we do nothing."

Huasha bowed and said something that sounded like what he had said before.

"But I am not a surgeon."

"This is not much more than a simple bloodletting," said Master Wu. "We are only letting water out from the area outside the lungs."

"You should do it, then."

"It is an important lesson for you."

"But, but ..."

"I will double your fee. Fourteen pounds of silver."

Again Koshyar felt he was being tricked. A man's life was in the balance, and Koshyar was being pressured into performing a surgery beyond his limited experience. The silver being offered was as illusory as before, but at the very least it would be a new technique he might gain, and so he steeled himself by thinking of the abbot as a goat.

Thus prepared, Koshyar took up the scalpel. The monks held down the seated abbot by his shoulders and arms. They began chanting.

"Where's the lancet?" asked Koshyar. When he had it, he wrapped it with a cloth so that the exposed point was as wide as his thumbnail.

"Hold this," he said, giving it to Master Wu, trading it for the scalpel.

Koshyar ran his fingers along the abbot's lower left ribs, found the spot between the ribs, and made the cut. Now he was committed, but his nerves flared up on him with the realization that this wasn't a goat he was treating; it was a man. Sweat streamed into his eyes, and as he handed over the scalpel, his hand trembled. Then he took the lance and drove it into the cut, up to the cloth.

"Here is the bowl," said Master Wu, "to catch the flow of empyema."

Koshyar held the bowl in place and removed the lance. Pus spurted out into the bowl.

Koshyar felt the sweat on his brow suddenly dry. His face remained impassive, but inside he said a prayer of thanks.

The discharge streamed, increasing whenever the abbot drew a breath. When the flow slowed to a trickle, Koshyar plugged the wound with a tent of raw linen, tying it with a cord.

Koshyar and Master Wu walked outside and examined the contents of the bowl.

"It is white and pure," said Master Wu. He bent closer and took a deep sniff. "It is not fetid, nor clotted." He looked Koshyar in the eye. "An excellent sign. I thank you for all your help."

Master Wu gave him a deep bow.

* * *

"Here is your token of payment, an Atlantean spark-jar," said Wu, handing the vase-sized object to Koshyar. The cylindrical ceramic item was surprisingly heavy, as if packed with lead. "Notice that the two leather caps cover metal posts—make certain that the caps remain in place, and keep metal objects away from it."

"And for this I will be given fourteen pounds of silver?"

"Yes, you have my word."

After Koshyar packed the artifact away, Master Wu said, "The daylight wanes. Won't you stay the night and leave in the morn?"

"Thank you, but no." Koshyar glanced around, taking in the landscape, and said, "This valley is a bright spot in a harsh land. Like the rest of the world, it is the work of Allah. It may not be as pleasing to the human eye as many other places, but it is the true art of nature.

"The giants, on the other hand, are the work of man. They challenge the work of Allah. They mar the beautiful art of this valley. They make one feel as if he is being watched not by Allah, but by a pair of devils. If they had been destroyed, the kingdom would not have fallen."

Master Wu thought for a moment, and then said, "There is no hope of healing without first draining the hatred."

To Koshyar this seemed like a non sequitur, and he shook his head in irritation. "More to the point," he said, "if the statues had been destroyed, your fellow countryman would not have come here, and thus he would have avoided getting two diseases."

At this, Master Wu smiled broadly. "Oh no, to the contrary—were the giants destroyed, the number of pilgrims would double, I'm sure!"

GHOST HEART OF SAN FRANCISCO

Old women get hot flashes, but old hippies get flashbacks.

That's what sixty-year-old Rice thought as streetlights under the afternoon sun foliated into palm trees swaying in a snowstorm of spider web strands. The crowds on both sides of the wide city street froze into marble statues, became shrouded by webs, evolved into coral reefs where birdmen flittered and twittered.

Rice's progressive bifocals seemed to be fogging up. Shivering, he turned up the collar of his denim vest, felt it brush against his gray ponytail, but then the vision snapped back to normal.

His visit to San Francisco had turned into

a "natural" acid trip, where the Summer of Love merged with the first months of the Obama administration, ghosts of past and present interacting, showing the way from the nightmare straight to Pepperland. The Bush Nightmare, to be sure, the bluest of the Blue Meanies, but now with the new dawn Rice could admit his own deep disappointment with the Clinton Collapse. Like a coalmine canary, Rice had fallen away in the '90s —like a wounded animal he had holed up in Big Sur for fifteen years, far from the corruption of compromise in the big cities.

But now he was back in a world refreshed, made new. Every morning he checked Google news and felt a pleasant espresso-like jolt upon seeing that Obama had not been assassinated. And as part of his new optimism he had driven his VW bus up to San Francisco for the festivities.

It was his first Gay Pride Parade, though. While he wasn't at all gay himself, he quickly warmed to the masculine agenda on display. Maleness, manly power, male style, male sexuality unlimited by the bonds of tepid conformity. A bold celebration of Man in a pussy-whipped nation.

Just as Rice felt this Tantric Epiphany, a float bearing a Village People tribute group was rolling up. They were singing the old hit tune "Y.M.C.A.," but the words were changed:

Why not be Gay?
Why not try Gay-hey?

You can get your pipes cleaned,
You can have a good time,
You can check out the other side!

Rice looked up at the cop, the Indian chief, the cowboy, the construction worker, the biker, and the soldier. He was grooving on that far out vision where such opposites as cowboys and Indians, blacks and whites, cops and construction workers, could all get along together, even if not literally getting it on together. This was the dream made true, post-racial, post-partisan. Perfectly Pepperland.

But then Rice got a weird vibe from the fake "Native American Indian" member of the group, who had stopped dancing and was staring at him intently. The man looked like he was flying the same LSD tab that Rice was on, his eyes so wide and black and acid clear, like wells reaching up to infinity, that Rice was afraid he would fall into them. And whoa, was that a gun in the guy's loin cloth?

No, he was just "happy." As gay as a Maypole.

It was too much for Rice, the way the guy was staring at him. He felt spots of heat across his face and body, as if a Blue Meanie heat ray were tagging him for the death blast. He unbuttoned the top of his long-sleeved tiedye shirt. Suddenly thirsty, he turned and started pushing his way through the dancing crowd, heading toward the concession tents, hoping to buy a drink. When he glanced back he saw to his surprise that the fake Indian had jumped off the stage and was pursuing him.

Alarmed, Rice ran into the first tent. There was one corporate frat boy face down on a table, his bare-butt being spanked by two burly bikers using a hairbrush and a ping-pong paddle. A couple of other corporate guys were videoing the whole thing, a mid-western twang to their giddy commentary on the bright red welts.

"Whoa, hey, there's a line," said one, laughing at Rice's sudden arrival.

"We got a couple minutes left on this," said the other.

"Instead of minutes, maybe it should be the number of smacks remaining?"

Rice saw the side entrance to the left and took it. He zigged and he zagged through the forest of cigar-store Indians, following a trail of wooden nickels. On the horizon the gigantic head of Iron Eyes Cody, the crying Indian, wept his glycerin tear. The wooden Indians were burning. Rice passed several smoldering teepees in different Dali landscapes before ducking into one at random.

"*Irasshaimasse!*" said a blonde woman in a Victorian maid outfit. "Would my lord like a cup of tea?"

"Yes, yes I would," said Rice, wiping the sweat from his brow with a red bandana. "Iced tea?"

"Oh, I'm so sorry! All we have is hot tea—"

She screamed as the fake Indian burst in.

* * *

He was listening. The man was talking, had been talking for a long time. They were standing in a tepee. There were two bodies on the ground, at their feet.

"*Will you find it?*" said the man. He was flickering.

"Yes," he said.

"*You have a helper.*"

"I do?"

"*Here is another one,*" said the glowing man. In his hand there was a scorpion. Its claws opened and closed. Its stinger dripped poison.

The shimmering man put the scorpion into Rice's belly.

* * *

Rice found he was sitting at one of the tables. A cup and saucer were in front of him. He reached for the cup, and the Victorian maid, sitting across from him, said, "Are you back this time?"

"Yeah." He sipped the tea and found it lukewarm. The tea was real, the maid was real. "What do you mean, this time?"

"You've been fading in and out."

"I have?"

She nodded, and said,"How do you feel?"

"I feel . . . fine. Stone cold sober, and before I was pretty trippy. But what happened?"

"I'm not really sure," she said. "But it was hella freaky."

"There was an American Indian?"

"Yeah, a guy dressed like that, but it was like he was possessed or something."

"Was he really on fire?"

"On fire? No, I don't think so, but wait—there was something like that. But like, what was it?"

"So he came in," said Rice, doggedly. "Then what happened?"

"He was saying all this stuff to us, hella crazy stuff, and then I like woke up on the floor."

"He said stuff?"

"He wanted us to find something. Very important, like a quest or something."

"Yeah, yeah!" said Rice, putting the cup down. "It was his heart, wasn't it?"

"I guess," she said, skeptical. She put a finger to her cheek and gazed up at the ceiling. "He kept like saying the word 'rock' in different languages, like he said 'Do the rock' in English, and he said *ishi*, which is Japanese for 'rock.'"

"Wait, he said *Ishi?*"

"That's what I said."

"As in 'Ishi, the Last of his Tribe'?"

"I guess," she said. "Is that some anime? Sounds like Miyazaki."

"No, he was an American Indian from around here. A famous one." Rice stroked his Fu Manchu mustache from the corners of his mouth to the edges of his chin. "A fake talking about the real."

"There was like, something about a red man dying to get out from inside the white man."

"This is crazy," said Rice, standing up. "I'm getting out of this."

But then he felt the scorpion under his skin, prodding at his liver.

"Don't go," moaned the maid, her face a mask of terror. "You have to . . . we have to . . ."

Rice dropped back into the chair with a thump that sent the scorpion away.

"So anyway, the ghost said to find this thing for him, but where is it?" said Rice. "Is it right here, buried on this spot?"

"Hey, I don't know. It would be pretty hard to get through the pavement here. But dude, if it isn't right here, then where in the City could it be?"

"He must have told us. Did he point to the ground or anything like that?"

"No, nothing like that."

"Tell me what he said again."

"He said, like, 'Ishi,' and that 'white man' thing, and all that rock stuff. 'Do the rock,' 'I do the rock'— oh my god!"

"Are you thinking—"

"He means Alcatraz!"

"—what I'm . . . well, yeah, you are. Obviously."

"We have to go!" she said, and she started to take off her clothing.

"Whoa, whoa!" said Rice. Already her pale neck

was exposed. "What are you doing?"

"I've got to change." She gestured toward a gym bag on the chair beside him. "Here, get it out for me."

In the gym bag he found a bright yellow training suit.

"But . . . but . . ."

Her shoulders were bare.

"You're gay so it doesn't matter."

Her clavicle and the upper slopes of her . . .

"I'm not gay!"

"Oh!" Her hands halted in their work, and then a blush lit her cheeks as she began refastening her costume. "So what, you're bi-curious?"

"Huh?"

"Um, looking for some bro-mance? Willing to try gay?"

"Hell no!"

"Well then, what're you doing at the Pride if you don't want a man date?"

"I came here for Obama."

"You got a woody for the President?"

"No! Just to celebrate."

"Well, this isn't a Fourth of July Parade, this is an identity event."

"So what, I can't go to the Saint Paddy's Day Parade if I'm not Irish?"

"No, you shouldn't go unless you want to get *blotto*."

"Yeah, all right," said Rice, his shoulders slumping in defeat. "I get it now."

"Innocence Lost."

Rice wanted a change of subject. Looking at the costume in the bag, he saw a safe topic. "Hey, I bet you look like Uma Thurman in this." He gave her a little smile. "You know, *Kill Bill*."

She flinched as if she had been slapped.

"What's your name, anyway?" she asked, coldly, straightening up so she towered over him, a frightening Maid of Discipline and Correction.

"Rice," he said, bewildered.

"I'm Ronnie," she said. "And I really hate *Kill Bill*, so don't bring it up again."

"All right."

"Let's go."

"Go where?"

"To Alcatraz."

"Oh, okay. My bus is parked over—"

"We'll take my Vespa, it's faster."

"Sure."

When they got to the yellow scooter, Rice couldn't believe what he saw.

"*This* is a *Vespa?*"

He had assumed it would be like the 50 cc model from *Roman Holiday,* but Ronnie's scooter was a hulking monster of at least 250 cc.

"Oh yeah. Racing model, customized."

"*Racing* model?"

"Google it."

"I'm goggling it now," he said, wiggling his glasses. She grinned at that.

For Rice it somehow fit with her scary alter-persona he had seen so briefly—it had been a tough female biker. The costume had been wrong, though, since that biker would never wear a frilly maid outfit.

She started it and told him to sit on the saddle behind her.

"Keep your arms around my waist," she said. "Don't grab my tits or you'll get some drama. And you don't want no drama."

Yeah, Biker, he thought.

They surged away like a rocket, weaving and swerving through the Pride Weekend traffic. Rice alternated between gasping and laughing as they raced along Van Ness, with *Born to be Wild* running through his body.

"I hate riding in a skirt," Ronnie yelled over her shoulder. "Hold it down, will you?"

So he had one hand on her thigh and the other around her waist as they gradually gained altitude. Rice thought it was pretty cool, like being in *Easy Rider* or something, except instead of Peter Fonda steering the chopper it was his sister, who looked like Uma.

"We're gonna turn right, and you gotta lean into it," she yelled. "Way into it."

"Okay!" he said, switching his grip so that his left arm was around her waist.

"Now," she said, putting the scooter over hard. Rice kept his eyes ahead, aware of the pavement flying by only inches away from his face.

They rose upright coming out of the turn. Now

they were blasting downhill, making it even more like a roller coaster. The scene was as pretty as a postcard, with a cable car coming up in the middle of the street, full of riders gasping and taking pictures of them through the rear window like they were movie stars.

Rice felt like a star. Ishi had made him the star, and Ronnie was just his helper, but still she was Best Supporting Actress.

It seemed like the scooter got airborne once or twice, then they made a left turn. The traffic on the new street was stopped by something ahead, so they made another left and that's when things really started to go crazy for Rice. He had a spiraling sensation of vertigo, silently screaming as he rotated round and round. A pagoda flashed by, chased by several dragons in lush Technicolor and pandas in crisp black and white. There was a crowded narrow alleyway, lots of sing-song shouting, followed by chicken feathers falling like fake snow.

Spellbound. 'It's Chinatown.' After a motion-blurred downhill part there was a white pyramid growing up like silly putty come alive, stretching to kiss the sky during a Hendrix solo, while the birds in flight formed a dark halo around it, ominous black cutouts in the bright blue sky.

"Hey, are you okay?"

They were no longer moving—they were parked on the street by a pier. She had gotten off the scooter already.

He wanted to tell her everything, express the incredible experience of pyramid, pagoda, and all that, the sense of watching a movie and being inside of that movie at the same time, and not just any movie, a great movie, and being an incandescent star in wonderland.

"It's like being in a Hitchcock film," he said, proud at having captured so much of it in just seven words, like a Zen koan.

"Huh?"

"Hitchcock."

"Dude, I thought you said you weren't gay."

"I'm not! Hitchcock isn't gay!"

"Sure sounds like gay porn to me."

"You're kidding."

"Nee-oop."

"Damn it, you better be," said Rice, rolling up his sleeves. "You don't know the name of a classic American director? How about *Vertigo*, *Psycho*—"

"You sound kinda psycho—"

"*The Thirty-Nine Steps*—"

"Maybe you could go back to a ten step program —"

"What a smart ass!"

"What a freaky geezer."

"I bet we could ask any foreign tourist, like those Japanese guys over there. I bet you ten bucks that they know who Hitchcock was."

"You're on." With long-legged strides she went straight to the cluster of middle-aged men, forcing Rice to trot.

"*Minna-san, konnichi wa!*" she said in a high, squeaky voice, which electrified the group into saying "oh" and "ah" in surprise. Ronnie followed with a barrage of Japanese, pointing to Rice once or twice, and the name "Hichu-kaku" once or twice. The Japanese consulted with each other in a huddle before one answered her in a barrage of his own.

Ronnie giggled and turned to Rice. "They like *anime!* These are my people."

"What's *anime?*" asked Rice.

Ronnie gave another helium-fueled word stream to the Japanese men and they became very excited.

"Hmm, well, I guess you're right," said Ronnie. "Ken-chan here tells me that Hitchcock is a lot like Satoshi Kon, one of my favorite anime directors."

Rice gave a little victory dance and said, "Arigato!"

"Quit fooling around," said Ronnie. "We have to get tickets."

The ticket booth had a sign saying that tickets were sold out, and looking at the schedule they saw that the next boatload to depart would be the last of the day.

"Oh no!" said Ronnie. "Now what will we do?"

"Maybe we can try again tomorrow?" said Rice, but he got a sick feeling below his stomach. "No, not tomorrow."

Ronnie looked on the verge of tears, the stern Maid of Discipline and Correction turned into the skinny little match girl dying in the snow. Desperate for a solution, Rice wracked his brains. "Maybe we could steal a jet ski?"

"*Annoooh,*" said Ken-chan, hesitatingly intruding into a fraught situation between colorful yet volatile foreigners. "You want go to Alcatraz Island? We have two tickets, extra."

"Oh, Ken-chan!" said Ronnie, her face radiant.

They spent the rest of their waiting time taking pictures of Ronnie and Rice, then pictures of Ronnie and each other, and finally Rice took pictures of Ronnie and the group.

"Hey," said Ronnie, "they think you're cosplaying!"

"Huh?"

"We look like two anime characters to them."

"Whatever," he said. "You're buying my ticket, 'cause I won the bet on Hitchcock."

"No way, dude," said Ronnie. "It's twenty-six bucks, like, over double."

"Okay, fine. So I pay sixteen bucks. I mean, you're not going to welsh on a bet, are you?"

"Well, about that," said Ronnie, folding her arms. "Ken-chan says he was a British director."

"Kah. All right, fine. A technicality." Rice took out his wallet, fished out the cash, and tried to hand it to Ken. Ken refused. Rice tried again. Ken was adamant about not taking money from either of them. Which meant that the two Americans were sort of "native guides," but Rice was fine with that—he thanked Ken and shook his hand.

Once all that was done, he asked Ronnie, "So what's this 'anime' you're all babbling about?"

"Japanese Animation."

"What?! Cartoons? Give me a break."

"Here's the funny thing," said Ronnie, in a conspiratorial way. "That tent where I was working? It was designed to get guys just like this group, as well as American anime fans who want a taste of Tokyo."

"What do you mean?"

"Maid Cafes are big in Tokyo. But get this— these guys came to the City but are too shy to go to the Pride, so they aimed for Alcatraz instead."

"Except for the two guys who didn't show."

"Hmm, right. Maybe those two are at the Pride, after all."

❊ ❊ ❊

The ride to the island would take about a half-hour. As they all sat together on the sight-seeing benches of the observation deck, Ronnie chattered away with her new friends, mainly about Japanese cartoons. Rice couldn't believe it— these were grown men, in their thirties at least. They were clean cut, with regular 9 to 5 office jobs that gave them enough money to travel to California. In short, they seemed like such straight arrow squares that he couldn't quite grasp this enthusiasm for cartoons, unless it was some kind of sexual perversion, a filthy Lolita-fetish lurking beneath their bland, inoffensive exteriors.

Then it all made sense. "Maid sense," in fact. Rice could imagine that they were in hog heaven with Ronnie. It was disquieting and distasteful to Rice, if it was really as depraved as he feared it was.

He looked out over the beautiful blue bay and wondered what the hell Alcatraz had to do with Ishi. There was no way Ishi would have gone there for a visit, since the place was a prison at the time, and it seemed impossible that he was buried there, in whole or in part.

They were just a few minutes away from the island when Ronnie suddenly turned and said, "Hey, they think you're my dad."

"No, no! I'd be proud, of course, but you could be my granddaughter."

"Well, hey, we should do that generation argument thing, like in *Flashback*."

"What's that?"

"Um, a movie? I thought you were, like, into movies?"

"I haven't seen that one."

"With Kiefer Sutherland and Denis Hopper."

"Never heard of Kiefer," said Rice. "Sounds like a yogurt drink—odd name for a girl."

"Hah. Well anyway, it has this scene where the old hippie is bitching about 'kids these days' and the young guy is firing back about the downside."

"Oh, like Jack Lemmon in *Save the Tiger*."

"I don't know. So anyway, look—you say 'Sexual Revolution,' and I say 'A.I.D.S.' You say

'Moon landing,' and I say 'Challenger disaster.' Like that, and we go back and forth until you win by saying the '60s are coming back again."

"'The '90s are going to make the '60s look like the '50s,'" said Ken, apparently quoting from the film.

"No that's a good point right there," said Rice. "I mean, what the hell happened? It's like *American Pie,* you know that one?"

"The movie?" said Ronnie. "Like in, 'One time at band camp . . .'?"

"Huh? No, not some movie, I mean the song. It really burns me up that the Clintons played it at their inauguration."

"How does it go? Sing a few lines and maybe I'll recognize it."

"All right, but I'll change the words."

A long, sad time ago
I can barely recall
How the peace dividend was ours to spend.
Instead of buying bomb and tanks
We could secure the future's thanks
With universal healthcare to the end.

But the summer made me queasy
With every compromise so sleazy.
Pepperland was off the page.
I couldn't hide my burning rage.

The evil men were all so snide.

Our leaders they had all just lied.
And something broke down deep inside
The Day the Promise Died.

("Oh, *that* one!" said Ronnie, clapping her hands with delight. "The Day the Music Died!")

(Rice launched into the chorus . . .)

I declare, where's my HillaryCare?
Drove my Honda over Fonda
'Cause she married a square.
And those corporate suits were singing laissez-faire
Saying, "Buddy pass the Camembert.
I'm gonna be a millionaire."

They arrived at the island just then, allowing Rice to quit while he was ahead.

The first thing they saw was the old graffiti "Indians Welcome to Indian Land" painted in red on the building by the dock, which gave Rice an "Oh yeah" moment, but Ronnie just had a blank look.

"The place was taken over by American Indians in the late sixties," said Rice. "I'm sure they'll cover that in the tour."

Most of the people just off the boat were listening to a state park ranger, forming a crowd by the building. Rice said, "We don't have time for that," and led his group on a beeline up the hill. They followed the signs to the cell house, where they waited in line in the shower room for the audio-headset tour.

Ronnie cracked some jokes about Soap on a Rope.

A woman ahead of them turned and, after looking Ronnie over, asked in a Russian accent, "You are Maid of Alcatraz?"

"I'm really a combat waitress—from the future!" quipped Ronnie.

"You can give to us details about Warden, yes?"

"Oh, no," said Ronnie, waving her hands in the flight of the hummingbird. "I'm not part of the island, I'm just dressed up. I am a tourist."

The woman sniffed and turned away.

"Well," said Rice, "now the shoe is on the other foot. A while back I was the tourist and you were the carny."

"Whatever," said Ronnie, casting an appraising glance around the place. "I wonder if I could actually get a job here, like she says."

"Sure you could," said Rice. "They don't pay, though."

"No pay, no play."

"So what's your story, anyway? Is Maid Waitress your full time job?"

"No, not hardly! I'm a college student at S. F. State."
"What's your major?"

"I'm majoring in Japanese and Hotel Management."

"Ah ha! I should've been able to guess that."

They got their headsets and, following the voices in their heads, wound through the prison. They peered into cells, learned about daring escape attempts, the isolation cells of D Block, celebrity prisoners like Al Capone and "the Birdman," and the near-fatal food fight over unacceptable spaghetti sauce. With Ronnie and Rice posing for staged photos at every station. But there was nothing about the Indian Occupation.

Their search for clues was getting nowhere, and after wandering from area to area, the two native guides became dispirited and grumpy, which dampened the enthusiasm of their four Japanese friends.

"This is not working out," said Rice. They had gone through the gift store and worked their way around to the highest point on the island again, near the lighthouse. "What's the connection? Why were we told to come here?"

"Well, we've run through all the gay porn jokes I can think of."

"I'm thankful for that, at least." They were between some ruins on the left and the lighthouse on the right, with a beautiful view of the city only a mile away across the water.

"There's still your connection, your Native American Indian connection."

"I guess, but I just don't get it," said Rice, shaking his head. "Ishi was never here, I don't think, and he died long before the occupation."

"Give me a few minutes," said Ronnie, pulling

out her smart phone. "I should've done this before."

"What, calling your boyfriend?"

"Doing internet research."

"You're kidding. On a phone?"

"Hush. I'll tell you what I get."

Rice sat down on a bench and gestured for the Japanese guys to do the same. He looked up into the blue sky at a patch of sketchy clouds that turned into the sand golden coils of a rattlesnake. It was breathing, the texture of the scales flexing, and the snake's head turned so it was looking directly at Rice. The tongue flickered out, sniffing the air. He could see the rattles at the tail, and they were still, not shaking.

The sky-snake was familiar to Rice. He had seen it on an acid trip back in '69 or '70. It was like seeing a forgotten old friend, and for a moment he was twenty again.

"Okay, Ishi," said Ronnie, snapping him back to 2009. "Last of his tribe . . . found in 1911 . . . thought to be age 51."

"This place wasn't even a Federal prison until the '30s, so it was still a military prison when Ishi was discovered."

"Brought to U.C. Berkeley to live as a museum exhibit. Died in 1916." She wrinkled her nose. "*Eeuw,* his brain was preserved for science."

"Wait a second—he was living as an exhibit?" said Rice. "My God, that sounds like Nazi stuff. And they took his brain? More Nazi stuff."

"It was by some guy named Kroeber, if that means anything."

"Hell yes it does! Famous anthropologist. His name's on one of the campus buildings." Rice shook his head in disgust. "Man, he probably built his whole reputation on the Nazi experiments he put Ishi through, during Ishi's life and after his death. We should've been protesting that, the evil rot at the root of the whole U.C. system."

"Huh," said Ronnie. "So you were a Berkeley protester back in the day?"

"Yeah."

"Wow, so you were a student there and everything?"

"Well, no . . . but let's keep on track. It smells like a conspiracy here if they aren't telling us about the Indian Occupation during the audio tour."

"Wasn't there a theater or something half-way up the hill? Maybe we should check it out."

"Might as well," said Rice, rising up slowly.

Ronnie said something to the Japanese men and the group started back toward the dock, heading up a bit to the summit and then down the hill. After the second switchback in the steep road, an ally opened up on the right with a signpost to the theater. They followed this down to a stark building that seemed more sinister and menacing than the cell house. They walked in the growing darkness as the sky narrowed to a shrinking strip above.

Entering what felt like a basement, Rice found

a hallway with doors on both the left and right. The first one on the left led to a viewing room for the orientation video. The second one on the left was similar, but in Spanish, as was the third one.

The hallway was a dead end. Across from the third viewing room was a display room on the birds of Alcatraz. Rice walked back toward the entrance, passing a couple more display rooms. He was about to boil over when he found that the last display room was a tiny viewing room for a video about the Indian Occupation.

There was nobody else in there, so Rice led the group to the front row of low seating-blocks and they all sat down to wait for the movie to start.

"What do our friends here make of all this?" asked Rice. "I mean, American Indians, occupation and stuff."

"We feel brotherhood with American Indians," said Ken. "We are related to Eskimo."

"Really?" said Rice.

"Yes! A Japanese scientist went to Alaska and he could understand their language. It was Japanese."

"Wow."

"Wait," said Ronnie. "Is this one of those kooky theories, like about how Genghis Khan was really Minamoto Yoshitsune?"

"But that's true," said Ken.

"Huh," said Rice. "Mongolians are really a lot like American Indians. I never thought about that."

Ken smiled and nodded. "And we Japanese also know what it is like to suffer American Occupation."

"Oh brother," said Ronnie. "You mean your *grandparents* did."

"No! Even today, American forces occupy my country."

"He's right," said Rice, but Ronnie waved him to silence because the video had started.

Rice found himself drawn deeply into the video. The archival clips put him directly back into the late sixties. *The first takeover lasted a few hours in 1964. The longer takeover started in November of 1969. The Warden's house was the most comfortable residence and became their headquarters. In May of 1970 the electricity was cut off. On one night in June, two devastating fires broke out, one destroying the officer's club, the other gutting the Warden's house and damaging the lighthouse.*

Rice was dimly aware of other people coming into the room, sitting in the rows behind him, but all of his senses and emotions were stretched out like the feathery fingers of a sea anemone. *In January the occupation leader's thirteen-year-old daughter fell from a height and died shortly thereafter. The leader, devastated by this tragedy, left the island. The occupation ended five months later.*

He could feel the triumph and the despair, he could taste the camp food and Kool-Aid, he could smell the pot smoke . . .

Rice sniffed a few times. He really could smell

pot smoke.

He glanced back and saw a bunch of young American Indians in jeans.

He snapped his head back to face the front. It was too weird. He told himself the punchline of that Lone Ranger joke, the one where Tonto says, "What do you mean *we*, pale-face?" and suppressed a giggle. He decided that they were just historical re-enactors, but still, he wondered that they would be smoking outside of a designated smoking zone, let alone smoking marijuana.

The lights went out and the video died.

"They cut the power," said one of the strangers in the dark.

Rice turned and said, "I have a question maybe you can answer."

"Sock it to me, chief."

"We're looking for Ishi's heart, or maybe his brain."

"Ishi, huh?"

"Yeah. Something of his was buried."

"Sure, I know."

"Can you take us to it?"

"It ain't gonna be easy, chief."

"We have to try."

"All right, let's go."

Rice stood up and headed for the door. Ronnie and the Japanese were still looking at the blank TV screen.

"Come on," said Rice.

"Huh?" said Ronnie, looking around in

surprise. "But . . . uh, okay. Sure."

Rice felt an oppressive weight lift off of him as he left the building. Following the American Indians up the incline, he counted them and found there were six. Three wore t-shirts, one had a vest without a shirt, and the last sported a faded blue work shirt. The tourists around them were ignoring the Indians, except for infants in strollers who stared and a toddler who pointed.

"Where we going, Rice?" asked Ronnie as they worked their way back uphill.

"I don't know, we're just following them."

"Who?" said Ronnie.

"The Indians," said Rice, pointing ahead.

"Oh, right."

They hiked up the switchbacks and in a few minutes were back at the spot between the ruins of the Warden's house and the lighthouse.

"This is the place?" asked Rice.

"Yep," said the American Indian in the work shirt, the lighthouse at his back.

"Huh," said Rice. "I was thinking maybe it was buried in the garden, or someplace with, you know, dirt." He tapped his heel on the pavement. "This is pretty hard to dig through with a shovel."

"You can't use a shovel for this job, chief."

"Well, then what do we do? Hold hands and sing *Kumbaya?*"

"Something like that."

"You're putting me on."

"Nope." He produced a pocket radio straight

from the '60s and turned it on.

"What's happening, Rice?" said Ronnie.

"Shh, he's telling me something," said Rice, but then he heard the first few bars of the song on the radio and gave a cough of disbelief.

"You know this song, chief?"

"Sure," said Rice. "It's a remake—"

"Good. You and your team have to perform it. Right here, right now."

"You've got to be kidding!"

"Nope."

"But . . . that song—"

"Yep."

"Is it okay if I change the words?"

"Sure, just don't mess with the background chant."

"All right." Rice turned to the others. "We— I am going to do another singing thing, and this time I need your help."

"Ooo, karaoke time!" said Ronnie, and the faces of the Japanese lit up. "What's the song?"

"It's way before your time," said Rice. "Now listen, you guys, I need you to sing. Ronnie can't sing it, this chant I'm going to teach you. It's for men only. Okay? It goes like this: *oo-ga chaka, oo-ga chaka, oo-ga chaka, oo-ga oo-ga oo-ga chaka . . .*"

"But what's it called?" said Ronnie in her most exasperated pout.

"It's *Hooked on a Feeling*," said Rice. "Okay, ready? Go!"

The Japanese tourists started their chant,

moving their arms to the rhythm as they got into the primitive, magical, masculine essence of it. Rice let them run a few measures, and then burst into song:

> *I just got this feeling,*
> *A grin from ear to ear.*
> *Girl, you have to realize*
> *We got a mandate here.*

(Ronnie giggled at that. The American Indians were chuckling, nudging each other and tapping their toes.)

> *When the people*
> *Vote the Left at last,*
> *That's when you know*
> *Everything's a blast —*

(Rice gestured the chanting to cut, then belted forth the primordial yell:)

> *Ah, ah-ah, ah-ah!*

(The American Indians each whipped out a kazoo . . .)
> *I woke up this morning*

(and blew forth the horn section accompaniment to the chorus.)

Pepperland is aborning
The President is ours!

(The American Indians stamped their feet twice for the percussive close to the chorus, then doubled over in laughter. Ronnie was doing a little dance. Ken was watching Rice, ready for his cue, but Rice shook his head and continued.)

He's a real Boomer,
The Sixties through and through.
But he will make that glory look
Like the Fifties, yes it's true!
When the people
(Rice cued the chanting to start.)
Vote the Left at last,
That's when you know
Everything's a blast —
(Rice cut the chanting, gave again the Tarzanic yell:)
Ah, ah-ah, ah-ah!
I'm hooked on a feeling,
(Kazoos: *Boo-boooo, boo-boooo . . .*)
Sky-high on believing,
(Kazoos: *Buh-buuh, buh-buuh*)
That Pepperland is here!
(*stomp-stomp*)

Rice looked around as he sang the chorus a second time. The kazoo-accompaniment was losing power since the Indians were laughing so hard. A crowd of tourists had gathered around to watch the spectacle, but many were pointing at the ruins, where a swirling smoke or dry-ice mist was boiling up from the gutted basement of the warden's house.

Then he saw a sudden movement in the sky, the rattlesnake. It was coming down towards the ruins, tail first, like an undulating lightning bolt.

Rice started the chorus again as the snake's tail entered the frothing fog, and just as he finished, the snake's head went under. He was taking a breath for another repetition when suddenly light blasted from the ruins. A glowing, red, pulsing heart came up from the mist. It rose slowly, but with each pulse it gained speed until it shot up into the sky, arching like a rocket. Then it exploded, forming a pink cloud.

The next thing Rice knew he was surrounded by park rangers who were talking into walkie-talkies, asking him questions, telling him that fireworks were prohibited at Alcatraz. Rice, Ronnie, and the Japanese men were herded away like a bunch of naughty kids taken to see the principal. It was all a big fat hassle, but Rice was too stunned or stoned to get belligerent about the typical fascist reaction.

❊ ❊ ❊

"What—what happened?" said Ronnie, holding her head.

"Are you back this time?" said Rice.

"Yeah. Wait, what do you mean, this time?"

"You've been fading in and out."

"I have?" She looked around at the concerned Japanese faces surrounding her.

Ken nodded, and said, "How do you feel?"

"Where are we?"

"This little holding area," said Rice. "They're shipping us out on the next boat. Mainly they were worried about you, I bet, but now that you're better, that's that."

"What do you remember?" asked Ken.

"Uh, I was, like, dancing? Yeah, a little *parapara Caramelldansen,* and you guys were like, singing. I was getting dizzy, and then I was like falling, only up, into the sky. And then there was like an explosion? Or maybe that came first."

"We'll say you were dehydrated," said Rice. "No, sun stroke, that's the ticket."

"But what *happened?*"

"Never mind what happened," said Rice. "The real question is, 'Was that *it?*'"

"Say what?"

"Well, I don't get what happened," said Rice, struggling for words, "or why it happened, or even why it would help, but I feel different. Right here." He put a fist on his beer belly. "Like, like as if Ishi is at peace now."

"Hey, me too!" said Ronnie, brightening up. "So, that was it? Okay, yeah, that feels right. But what . . . what was it?"

"I don't know," said Rice. "Maybe some American Indians had liberated Ishi's heart from Berkeley or wherever it was being held, and they buried it under the basement of the warden's house. Because it was their great victory. Sort of like 'Bury my heart at Wounded Knee.'"

"But, but—what about those Native Americans?"

"They got away."

"How?"

Rice grinned, and bit back making an Indian joke.

"They were toward the lighthouse, right?" he said. "And there's the fireworks at the Warden's house, so we're all looking in that direction, the opposite way. Then they run off, maybe as if they're going to get help, but they just vanish."

"But, like, the rangers know who all the re-enactors are, right?"

"Supposedly, but they act like they don't know of any Indians like the ones we described."

"So, what—they were tourists, who changed?"

"Yeah, real pranksters. Fireworks and quick change artists—like ol' Coyote himself."

* * *

Park Rangers escorted them down to the dock. While waiting in the line to board the ferry, they overheard snatches of conversation related to the strange event—people seemed to think it was an anti-government protest, against the bailouts or something.

Once on the boat they all went up to the top deck. Ronnie noticed the pink cloud and pointed it out to the others. It approached San Francisco, seemingly against the prevailing wind, while a steamy white cloud was hovering low over the city. The ferry left the dock and followed along the same track as the pink cloud, but so much faster it seemed they would soon catch up. The big cloud was flickering with lights and shadows. An image resolved and began to move.

"Hey, look!" said Rice. "It's the spanking tent."

The cloud showed a movie of the Midwestern tourist getting his consensual corporal punishment, then zoomed in on his face, the burning blush of a secret fantasy being fulfilled.

Ronnie looked up from playing with her phone. "Now *that's* bi-curious, like I've been trying to tell you," she said. Lowering her gaze to the phone, she added, "Call it exhibit A, or 'Paddle to the Sea.'"

"How can they do that?" said Rice. "I mean, not the spanking part, but projecting it onto a cloud like that."

"I don't know," said Ronnie, shrugging. "It's like YouTube in the sky. Technology is like that. Maybe they use lasers. Maybe the cloud is man-made—yeah, it must be."

"It must be 'cloud computing,'" said Ken, which made Ronnie laugh uproariously, while Rice could only shrug.

A new image took form of four men engaged in two pairs, prompting Rice to say, "It's like your TV in the sky is stuck on the porn channel."

"Oh!" said Ken, his eyes bugging out before he looked away.

Rice squinted at the foursome in the cloud. One was black, one was white, and two were . . .

"I guess we know where the missing members of the tour group went," he remarked.

"Wait a minute," said Ronnie. She was surprised when they all looked directly at her, then she glanced up at the aerial orgy they were avoiding. "Oh, I get it." She looked back down at her phone. "Anyway, it says here that Ishi's brain was given a proper burial years ago."

"Well, we didn't say that was his brain, it was his heart."

"Only they don't say anything about his heart being missing, taken for science."

"Maybe it was a big secret."

"I think the Native American Indians would've raised hell about it."

"Unless they were the ones with the secret."

"So wait, the Native American Indians got a hold of the heart in 1916, held onto it for like fifty years, and then buried it on Alcatraz?"

"Yeah, something like that," said Rice, standing up to stretch his legs. "I mean, what else makes sense? And why would Ishi tell us to go to Alcatraz, if that wasn't the case?"

Ronnie, looking up at Rice, saw something on the porn cloud.

"Look!" she said.

"Now what?" muttered Rice. Rather than porn, there was an American Indian, a man in his fifties, smiling and waving. "Ishi?"

The small pink cloud from Alcatraz collided with the white cloud, and suddenly another man was there with Ishi. They embraced, and began to dance into the sunset, sashaying to the tune of *I Left My Heart in San Francisco.*

"Well now," said Rice.

"See, I was right," said Ronnie. "It wasn't *his* heart, it was his *boyfriend's* heart."

"I guess," admitted Rice, grudgingly. "It just seems to raise more questions."

"Like what?"

"Like . . . oh, I don't know," said Rice. "Who was that guy, anyway?"

"Who knows."

"Couldn't see his face, just the back of his head," said Rice. "Maybe he was American Indian, but maybe he was white."

"Maybe he was Asian," said Ronnie. "Maybe he was African-American."

Rice laughed. "You're right. It's Frisco, baby. Baghdad by the Bay."

PARADISE AXIS

1. At The Great Ziggurat Of Mars

"We do not wish to recreate Terra's nightmare of flesh-eating savagery," said Duchess Raccoon (Stage 351) through her bead veil. "Terraforming hath gone far enough, perhaps too far."

A dozen people sat around the circular conference table in the Animal Chamber. Ten were aristocrats of recent stages: the non-aristocrat being Wilframia Terran, tagged as a non-citizen by the blue badge on her black turtleneck. Her dark hair was cut in a short bob and she wore the pinstripe jodhpurs of a common laborer.

"The land animal ecology of Mars is out of balance," said Wilframia. "The gatherers and the browsers have had no predators in their twenty-five years. These herbivores are overtaxing the plant ecology as well as becoming a nuisance to farms and cities."

Count Prairie dog (Stage 352) patted at his hair, smoothing an imagined blemish to the silver beehive.

"If one is so eager for Terra-like conditions," he

drawled, "why not return to Terra?" The snide took on an edge of menace. "It could be arranged."

Wilframia had never seen the count in person before. She saw he was arrayed in the highest fashion, with a ruffle lace collar and buckskin jacket. The uniform of new aristocrat males, but his personality was far from "noble."

"Aseph, wouldst thou forcefully repatriate third generation Martians rather than allow wolves on Mars?" asked Baroness Firefox (Stage 352) from the other side of the table.

"Wolves, wolves—must there be wolves?" said Duchess Raccoon. "Why not dogs instead? There must be plenty of feral dogs already at work on the problem of imbalance."

Gaekwar Woodgrow (Stage 342) now spoke with the voice an aged man from an old noble house (Stage 282), cultured yet informal: "D'yee know, one of the reasons why I arranged for our meeting to be here at the Great Ziggurat was to impress upon all participants that the Plan was carved in stone, and carved in no uncertain terms."

The wall behind him was covered with a 4,000-year-old mural done in a vivid cavepainting style. This artwork radiated the awe and mystery of the niche chain through the sacred animals of the forest: nimble gatherer, big browser, swift chaser, burly hunter, silent pouncer, laughing scavenger, graceful grazer, scary intimidator, and frightful seizer.

"Four world-empires have risen and fallen

since that time, but over all, through glory times and dark ages, the Plan has been implemented—may I remind us all that the very first Unmasking Day came only in Kasei 92, thirty-five years ago? We stand on the verge of completion—only eight Stages remain, as few as 70 years if we can avoid further delays. We must not falter now."

"Pardon one in advance for accidental rudeness," said Count Prairie dog, "but doth the oration of the high caste speaker possess a purpose?"

"Count Prairie dog," said Wilframia, "it is clear that Gaekwar Woodgrow is talking about the animal food chain sequence, how it rests upon the plant niche pyramid. Ten tree units feed one gatherer, like your namesake the prairie dog; five grass units and five tree units feed one browser. Such is as we have on Mars now. But ten herbivores feed one carnivore, ten units from carnivores, herbivores, and plants feed one omnivore, and so forth, raising and broadening the pyramid." She found the gaekwar looking at her with something more than intellectual approval.

The duchess, tilting her head back so that the beads of her veil nearly bounced off her chin, said, "The niche in question is already filled with wild dogs."

"Duchess Raccoon," said Gaekwar Woodgrow. "While your idea has a certain amount of the spirit of the Plan, it does so only by ignoring the letter of the Plan. See here, this is the Hesperian ideogram sequence for the category: 'it chases,' 'it kills in a group or alone,' 'eats living flesh and dead flesh,' 'body mass less than one Earthman,' and most pertinent, 'like a dog but not a dog,' with 'not domesticated' apparently added for emphasis. The Lemurian, Hyperborean, and Yssian texts are virtually identical—the prototypical chaser as envisioned by those who built the Great Ziggurat and carved the Plan was 'wlkwo,' 'wlpo,' 'lupo,' 'lukwo,' all known to us as the Terran wolf."

"There is a wildness absent from the current arrangement," said Baroness Firefox. "I doubt that the ancients envisioned the overcrowded petting zoo that Mars has become."

"But the wolf is such a dread beast!" said another noblewoman. "Murdering old women, torturing little girls—"

"Pardon me, Molua," said the Duchess Raccoon. "I believe we may be near the end of it. Gaekwar Woodgrow, let us suppose that the chaser society is correct in their claim that the herbivore population is now too large. If things are as bad as that, should we not speed up the process and introduce the next stage as well, the hunter-omnivore?"

"The notion has some merit—"

"Then in the spirit of compromise, we will acknowledge the imbalance, they will acknowledge that the feral dog population has already taken the chaser niche, and we resolve to introduce hunters in order to restore balance."

"So," began Wilframia. "In overseeing the next stage of implementing the Plan, the honorable and ennobled societies of gatherer and browser are going to skip the wolf and add the bear, a creature that can prey upon the wolf?"

"If you like to see it that way, yes. There is no over-riding reason why we must have such dangerous creatures roaming our forests, and philosophically we are vehemently opposed to it. Dying of starvation, even if it comes to that, is infinitely preferable to being chased down and killed."

* * *

The representatives of the Paradise Axis left the chamber first, donning their animal-faced air masks and cycling through the airlock. By pre-arranged signal Baroness Firefox ordered her pro-chaser group to engage in light talk only.

Now that the meeting was over, Wilframia began to fume. The chaser society had been stonewalled again, for a fifth year. They had been passed-over, leap-frogged by the embryonic hunter society. Stage 353 was being turned into a sham, with the chaser society made into a pariah caste.

All they wanted was advancement, and for most of them that was merely citizenship. Her face blazed a scarlet flush as she was sorry for herself, then angry for her father, and finally enraged for her grandfather. Lured away from the tired Old World for a new life on bustling Mars, her grandfather had arrived in time to participate in Stage 350, the first Unmasking Day, but membership in that Stage was only open to the Kasei caste. A caste-restricted Stage had never been done before, but at the time it seemed like a harmless, one-time-only affair; a fitting gift for the people who had ended the centuries-long Age of Wars and established a universal state in Greatvalley.

The chaser society continued their social noises as they gathered by the airlock to put on their own masks: a dryad, a dragonfly, the reddish vulpine mask of the baroness, the gaekwar's satyr, and Wilframia's plain one. They passed through the lock in threes, then climbed the ladder up through the trapdoor and out onto the flat summit of the ziggurat.

An unparalleled view of Nightmaze province greeted them, a panorama of ancient monuments lit by early morning sunlight, rendered in the sharp, distance-crunching clarity granted by the very thin atmosphere of altitude 10 km. Fifteen kilometers west of the towering ziggurat, across an icy plain dotted by fir and spruce, squatted the massive sky-staring stone face of an early Elysian priest-king, still trying to ward off the space invaders who had long since come, conquered his empire, and then mostly gone. To the south were the canyons that gave the province its name, filled with cliff-cities established as the capital bailiwick of the Alien Requilibrium, still housing the Voidan elite a few millennia after that empire's collapse. To the east lay the maglev track leading to Greatvalley. To the north was a domed tourist-town, last stop of the line to the port at Mt. Peacock. Around the ziggurat itself clustered diminutive pyramids, obelisks, columns, and spheres, each celebrating the completion of one Stage or another.

The society of chasers began walking down the ziggurat's long spiraling ramp, talking in pairs through wires that connected their masks. Their elaborate coiffures prevented the men from wearing hoods, so their servants held umbraziers overhead, providing a personal cone of heat against the below-freezing temperature.

The side of the ziggurat on their right was divided into panels, engraved with detailed instructions, repeated in four extinct languages, outlining the last stages in the transformation of a cold, dead world into a vibrant twin of Terra in her prime. Since the axis members had turned the first corner and were out of sight, the chaser society felt free to salute the panel dedicated to their own quest.

Further down the north face the baroness said to Wilframia, "Let us visit the demigod, shall we?" She gestured and the party filed through the narrow passage into the ziggurat and entered the Nitrogen Chamber, their entourage stopping to guard the portal. Here the walls were covered with diagrams and formulae related to the nitrogen problem. After the Nitrogen Solution (Stage 280) had been effected by the Argyre Directorate, the chamber had been retrofitted with a silver sepulcher for the demigod and a cinerarium for his six followers. All of the visitors knelt briefly at the foot of the centuries-old tomb except for the gaekwar, who gave the Argyre-caste salute in an offhand way.

A team of uplander security specialists disguised as janitors approached, their huge chests housing lungs that allowed them to breathe here without masks. They quickly scanned each member with handheld detectors, signaling a find on Wilframia's blank mask as well as on the dragonfly mask. Wilframia simulated a huge sigh, and then swept her mask off in exchange for a clean one handed to her by a janitor; the dragonfly affected a sneeze and exchanged his. The bugged masks were put into a case where recorded conversations began "Why such a big sigh?" and "Do you need a tissue?"

"Finally," said the baroness, talking to Wilframia across the secure line.

"And here I was thinking that my lady was *paranoid* when we made all those recordings," said Wilframia.

"You underestimated Raccoon," said the baroness as the group went back outside to continue their descent down the ramp. "She is a natural military leader and will seek every advantage. They must have planted the bugs on their way in or out. In any event, the meeting went nearly as badly as we feared it might."

"That Count Prairie dog!" spat Wilframia. "My father, blocked from joining the Gatherers, then the Browsers, was assured of an automatic place in the Chasers. And here we are! They are forming a new caste at the lower end, a caste of common citizens, and turning us non-citizens into an outcaste!"

"It may be," said the baroness. "Yet their scheme seems unusual, since the other castes were added at the top. But you must watch out for Count Prairie dog—he delights in causing pain, as opposed to our Woodgrow, whose interests are more . . . amatory."

"I saw him staring at me," said Wilframia.

"Oh yes," said the baroness. "Lecherous old scoundrel. He is in his fifties and you are barely ten—well, I should talk, I'm twice as old as your brother, and he is my gardener. But look here, Willie, we need Woodgrow, yet his attention wanders so much that, well, he is distressingly easy to bribe with pleasures of the flesh, and as such he could betray us. So. You will have to manage him. Once his desires are met, he will drift."

"I understand." They turned the corner and began descending the east ramp.

"The duchess will be working at influencing

him," said the baroness. "Through surrogates, of course! Still, we need him solidly with us for the next hundred days."

"Two zodes!" said Wilframia. "That will be Winter, no, mid-Winter. It seems too long to play patty cake, but also too short to complete our goal. Do you really think we can do it by the end of the year?"

"We must," said the baroness. "We simply must."

A hand fell on Wilframia's left shoulder and she turned to look into the satyr's mask. He plugged his wire into her socket and said, "Mind if I cut in, Muchumma?"

"Not at all, my dear," said the baroness, reaching for her wire. "In fact I should be mingling." She unplugged and drifted back.

"Now Willie—may I call you Willie?"

"Yes, my lord."

"I propose that we get acquainted on a private tour of the remaining three chambers. Here, let's just go into the Chamber of Trees right here . . ." The rest of the party, save one escort, continued on without them.

Because the Chamber of Trees had been defaced millennia earlier it was more like a cavern, one that had the only "stalactites" on Mars. While his manservant guarded the entrance, the gaekwar pursued Wilframia through this darkened and stony grove, but she deftly turned his advances. They went outside and down the ramp to the next room, the Ecopoiesis Chamber, which was all about comets directed into the world, thickening the atmosphere and adding surface water, creating the Boreal Ocean of the north as well as the land-locked Argyrean Sea to the south. Here the gaekwar was promising her all sorts of things, and fondling her through her cold-weather clothing, but still she denied him. They went outside and descended the ramp to the first room, the Virgin Mars Chamber. Here, finally, amid the sand and rocks, she took the matter in hand.

2. Training To Be Wild

The "office" was a small, cluttered room right next to the "pit" arena. It felt crowded to Wilframia with only a desk and two chairs. Sawdust covered the floor, adding a woody spice to the doggie smell, and the din of the kennels was only slightly muffled by the closing of the office door.

"They've been raised by humans," she said, trying to be cool and in control to dispel the bungling chaos of the kidnapping. "So we want them to be trained to fear humans, and to fight animals."

"Yibe," said Idared, a big woman with light-brown hair and a rosy complexion. "I can do that. Get him can kicky and then ark him just this side of the dusties. Ab him, put the sense of fear in him, without deebling him."

'Ab,' that is 'beat,' thought Wilframia,

translating the rural dialect. *'Deebling' must be 'crippling.'* Aloud she said, "The tab—they say that wolves have a certain kind of strike. They, uh, hop up and slash down. It would be best if you could teach them how to do that."

"Uh-huh," said Idared. "After we get the basic fisterin' and stringin' down, then we will take up the finer points of stiff hatting. But what do they chiggle?"

"'Chiggle'?"

"You know, get gorm in guts." Idared made a gesture for eating.

"Oh! We will keep you supplied with, ah, varmints. Live critters for them to kill and feed on. Small at first, like squirrels and raccoons, rabbits. Bigger animals later."

"Aplenty bahl," said the trainer. "But it'll be a heelch of grasks, booker cats, and belkeeks to keep two wolves alive, and that's the earth."

"We can only pay you—"

"Hold up now," said the trainer. "You've been harpin' a heelch, but you've been hiding a heelch more. I ain't tuddish! I watch the greeley and I know that some wolves have been stolen. So first up, whose side are you on, Paradise or Chaser?"

Wilframia's blood ran cold.

"Chaser," she said.

"That's right," said Idared. "Sounds like the earth, because otherwise why would you be keeping them alive in secret instead of stringin' them in public? Only how come the greeley says that Paradise tweeds took them?"

"We made it look that way," said Wilframia.

"So you sharked them good," said Idared. "But the highheels are looking around, eebling everything and everyone because of how that priest got joe macked and wound up in the hospital. How much could I get from Argyre caste if I told them?"

"Nothing," said Wilframia. "We are already paying them for the priest's injuries."

"How much could I get from the Paradise tweeds if I told them about you?" said Idared.

"I don't like the sound of this," said Wilframia.

"I bet they'd give me more higs than you."

Wilframia stood up and moved toward the door.

"If you shy and pike now then I'll have no other choice," said Idared.

Wilframia, reaching for the doorknob, whirled around instead. "Then quit your—*harpin'*—and tell me what you want!"

Idared snorted.

"Earth is, I don't want higs," she said. "I want what you call 'social advancement.' I want to get up and away from the bottom, from the dirty necks and the deejirs. So you tell me this, if I throw in with you, ott for Stage 353 night and day, then how high can I get?"

"Higher than a mountain top," snapped Wilframia, and the next phrase, so often used in comedies of rustics, naturally followed: "*Higher 'n a billy goat.*"

Idared grunted as if she'd just been punched in the stomach, but then she burst out laughing, big white teeth showing. Wilframia blushed, remembering too late that in dialect the phrase meant "to be very drunk."

3. Interview With A Voidan

The funicular train finally came to a shaky stop. Wilframia followed the passengers out into the Voidan cave-city of Eboncliff.

Seeing it up close for the first time, Wilframia felt a shudder pass through her. The layout was exactly like that of a cave-city on the open valley wall, but where those places were bright and airy, this canyon was dark and gloomy. The three split-towers stretching nearly 200 meters from cavern floor to ceiling looked like blight-covered brobdignag trees, split open to reveal disease-hollowed cores.

She double-checked her notes and walked toward the west tower. The promenade had no trees or hedges, but there were marble statues. Strolling along were the silent Voidans, indispensable remnant of the Alien Requilibrium, each an ovoid riding on the shoulder-saddle of a headless. Mount and rider together looking like a giant-headed humanoid. Wilframia had not seen so many Voidans since her last visit to the Bureau of Motor Vehicles.

The tower elevator was normal inside, which was a great relief. The corridor she exited on was standard, too. She knocked on the door indicated by her notes and the portal was partially opened by a headless who blocked the way. His ears were upright and facing forward at the level of her eyes. Wilframia looked down into his face, located in the center of his chest. The goat-like eyes blinked, the mouth beneath them was a small line: the headless said nothing.

"H-hello, I'm Wilframia Terran. I've brought some things for . . ."

The two meter tall humanoid opened the door fully.

"This way please, honored guest," it said in a surprisingly soft voice.

She stepped past him and into the living room. Half of the room was taken up by a large elevated aquarium, which had room enough for many Voidans but at the moment held only one, who was partially submerged. Its coppery visor was pointed in her direction.

"Welcome to my domicile, cousin," said the speech synthesizer mounted on the glass. Wilframia could now see that a few of the Voidan's dozen spiny face-framing antennae were inserted into a communicator. "At last we meet in the flesh." The Voidan held its left hand up and waved the fingers in greeting. "Please call me Riv."

"Hello, cousin?" The communicator transmitted her words as impulses to Riv's antennae.

"But of course," said the voder. "We share ancestors, we are both of Terran stock, in contrast to my servant, whose species originated at a different star. This is your first time in a void dweller's home, I take it? I hope it is not too disorienting."

Like turtles in their shells, the Voidans had a protective casing for all vital organs. But unlike turtles, they never stuck their necks out. They could not: at the forward end of the ovoid body was the neck-less head where two saucer-sized lenses, rather like the dual headlights of a motorcycle, covered the face, giving Voidans a robotic look.

"Yes," said Wilframia. "I mean no, it isn't too disorienting. I brought the things . . ."

The Voidan made a puffing sound from the blowhole on its top/back and sank a bit in the water.

"Yes, the unmentionables," it said. "Are you certain I cannot interest you in refreshments, tea, fruit juice, or the like? All right then, we move onward at a brisk pace. Dispense with all preliminaries, consider them done. Now please remove the articles of clothing and let me see what you have."

"*What?*"

"Remove the artifacts. Place them on the table there so that I may view them." As she did so the Voidan summoned the headless to attend, then began examining the things Wilframia put on the table.

"Some jewelry," said the voder-voice. "A talisman of some sort. A tool. A wood sample, another wood sample, a charcoal sample. A bracelet. Lascar, move that bracelet over."

Wilframia watched carefully, trying to see if the Voidan showed any preference for the resources over the artifacts.

"Let us take a closer look at the talisman, shall we?" It stopped talking for a moment, its coppery lenses directed toward the item. After a puff of air from its blowhole, it began to talk again. "A pyramid. Turn it please." The Voidan was again motionless for a moment, then gestured for the thing to be turned again.

"An elongated pyramid, with three sides," said the voice. "Cousin, you have a face, what do you make of that portrait?"

Wilframia made a pretense of looking, but she already knew the image well: a human face with squinting eyes and a tongue protruding from its grimacing mouth. "It is scary."

"What does it seem to be saying?"

"Something tastes very bad."

"Yes, good," said the Voidan. "I think I can see that, too. Probably a ward against grave robbers, or against evil spirits. Common in primitive cultures across time and space."

After another contemplative pause, the Voidan said, "Your gift exceeds my expectations. To avoid disequilibrium I must recalibrate my reciprocation." Another pause. "The party you represent is experiencing a revenue shortfall. My initial gift was to be funds, which would temporarily alleviate the situation. A short-term solution. Your long-term goal is to overcome or evade your antagonists. You have told me that you have reason to believe that collusion and conspiracy took place in Stage 352. If this could be documented it would provide powerful leverage, but the evidence, if it exists, is hidden behind a thorny hedgerow of procedural safeguards.

"So I propose to set the monetary gift aside as seed money for R&D on this topic. I will personally use it and establish a paper trail of my path into the maze."

Wilframia saw this as a ploy to avoid paying, even though the offer sounded very interesting in principle. "Give me half the money," she said.

"What?"

"Give me half of the money, use the other half to investigate, like you said."

There was a silence punctuated by puffing and blowing noises. "You drive a hard bargain. We will do as you have said, but now with the aforementioned seed money I am buying in to your program—should you succeed, I will exercise social advancement."

They agreed to this.

4. The Gaekwar Woodgrow

Marsyas Daksha Marsyasides, the Gaekwar Woodgrow, caught himself trembling in anticipation of the coming assignation with his "pet Willie."

Look at you, he chided himself. *Quivering like a schoolgirl. You aren't in love, are you?* But then he relented and let the feelings surge through him, giddy, exhilarating, and erotic. *Perhaps I am. Ah, but whatever it is, what a wonderful feeling. Life!*

Dasya the butler escorted Wilframia into the study. Here she was: small and dark, seemingly soft and helpless as a waif. But no, in truth she was iron to his silver, a small hammer that was pounding him into some as-yet-unknown shape.

"Hello there, Willie," he said after he dismissed Dasya.

"Hello, my lord," she said with a bow as the robot left the room.

"Yes, that's right—we shall have to teach you how to curtsey," he said. "Important little detail for society." Inwardly he smiled, thinking *put her in her place.*

She blinked.

"Is this why I was invited here today?"

"No, of course not."

"Still, there is no time like the present," she said. "It shouldn't take too long—why don't you teach me now."

"No, some woman should teach you. My sister is not at hand, and it would be indelicate to ask my wife—well, you should ask Muchumma to help you next time you see her."

"Yes, my lord."

"Take a look at this," he said, gesturing to the desk behind him. "I think you will be pleased."

She stepped over and looked down at the large piece of paper covered with intricate markings. "What is it?"

"A map of my estate," he said. "Here are the buildings, where we are right now. But out here, in the forest, along this trail for a few kilometers and then we come to this." He tapped an oval drawn on the map. "The pen!"

The hoped-for response of her pleasure did not come.

"*Pen?*" she said, brow furrowed in puzzlement.

"Yes, the acclimatization pen," he said. "For the wolves, yes?" The light was dawning on her face as he continued. "They spend a few thirtnights in there, maybe a zode, and then we let them out. At which point they go into my forest and multiply."

"How do we feed them?" asked Wilframia, poring over the map. "We don't want them to get used to people."

"Dead animals are put in," he said. "Deer and elk killed on the road. Animal Control trucks will bring them here. But there are no worries about habituating them to humans—it just does not happen. They are not *dogs*, after all." Her face clouded at that. "By the way, how are the wolves?"

"Badly beaten," she said.

"What do you mean?"

"Physically beaten."

"Why, what happened?" cried Marsyas. "Did Axis agents—?"

"No, we did," she said, and then she told him about Idared's program.

"You stupid, stupid girl," said Marsyas. "You have weakened them for no good purpose, perhaps you have crippled them."

"No, they are fine," she said, her voice hinting at doubts. "Just bruised." He took a breath but she held up her hand. "Enough, not another word, they are fine. Now take me to this pen."

"What, right now?"

"Yes," she said. "I have to see it."

"But Willie—"

"Right now."

They drove an off-road vehicle up the dirt road and into the forest. After a while they came to the end of the road where they found a prefab hut, a trio of hovercycles, piles of steel pipes, and rolls of fencing mesh. At the edge was an upright section of fence, a wall perhaps three meters long, enclosing nothing.

"That's *it*?"

"My dear, construction of such a thing takes time. We are surrounding a few hectares, after all. Holes must be dug, posts must be cut and placed, and so forth. This section is just a test piece."

"It looks too low," she said. "They are from Terra, they can jump really high."

"But notice how the fence angles in at the top," countered Marsyas. "The height is fine, the angling inward means it is perfect."

"When will it be ready?"

"Soon, soon," said Marsyas. "The materials are here, the workers are hired—being hired. In a thirtnight it will be done and ready for the wolves, your pair and some of the other pairs."

"Other pairs?"

"Forget that I said that, since secrecy is paramount," said Marsyas. "But remember that we are trying to foster a wolf *pack*. Pairs or threesomes released will not work. We need at least ten or twelve, functioning together as a team."

Wilframia looked out over the land, taking it all in. Her face softened, her eyes began to sparkle. After a few moments he asked her, "Are you pleased?"

"Yes."

"So perhaps you would be willing to chase me down and force me to do unspeakable things?"

"Yes," she said. "But only because you have pleased me. If you disappoint me I will disappear."

His senses quickened as he thought: *Oh, look at her! She is like some grave Artemis, some goddess of the hunt!* Then off he bolted, a sprightly old man running into the forest.

She counted to 30 and then began her pursuit.

❉ ❉ ❉

The days rolled by: Apsuday, Meganday, Tiamatday. The members of the Fenris/Laurentia cell argued among themselves. Keeping the wolves isolated from the humans that they must fear meant they had no one to relax with or form any kind of bond with. The trainer's familiar pattern of breaking the animal and then nurturing it as a surrogate parent was not carried beyond the first part. With no rest period, the wolves were on edge most of the time, another factor pushing them toward psychological disorder. In theory all of this was good, in practice it was muddy, bloody, and increasingly fraught with doubt.

The police detectives were closing in on the Fenris/Laurentia cell, but Riveter was able to call on his Kasei contact to create a temporary bubble of safety around them. Unfortunately the public was not cooling down on the subject; to the contrary, it was heating up. Citizens who were not directly involved in Stage 353 were nonetheless gravitating towards either the Paradise Axis or the chaser society. With demonstrations and counter-demonstrations, the population was becoming galvanized, polarized: the indifferent middle was vanishing. Which put pressure on the police.

The days rolled by: Merkday, Joveday, Veneday. The sun reached its northernmost point in the constellation of the Snake-Holder on Ophiuchus

22, marking the arrival of Winter in the Southern Hemisphere, and then it began its long journey South. A minor news item about "Trog Flu" in a *homo erectus* reservation on the North Rim of Greatvalley gained momentum, becoming a major story "Trog Flu Hits Sapiens," and then, "Greatvalley Plague!"

5. Flight

The tiltprops revved up, the Sakura heliport dropped away, the plane was airborne. Wilframia nearly wept with relief as all the tension of the last twenty days was eased: the oval pen was ready, the wolves were being carried to it. They were escaping the police dragnet, and once at the pen all would be safe on private land. She thought of all the painful mishaps, the terrible mistakes, the bad luck. She thought of her brother Wolfgang so recently dead of the plague. The tears fell.

Idared and her husband Harris sat one behind the other in the seats to the right and across the aisle from her, their faces now close to the windows, excited by the novelty. Wilframia had flown this route several times in the last two thirtnights and the novelty was gone, except for the cargo—she looked down the aisle to the two big live-animal containers, strapped down securely.

For three hours they flew down Greatvalley, traveling East by Southeast and covering two thousand kilometers. They landed to refuel at a small town on the South Rim, just below the 6 km "air mask level." People fleeing Greatvalley in ground vehicles or on foot had inundated the town, normally a sleepy little place.

Their pilot got up, stretched his arms. "We will make this as quick as possible, but there is enough time to walk around, grab a bite to eat." The door was located in front of Wilframia's seat. The pilot opened it, cranked down the short ladder, and exited the plane. Idared and Harris followed, to stretch their legs and get food.

Wilframia closed the door after they left and kept a watch through the small window at her seat, looking out from under the plane's high wing. A fuel truck came along but went past, going somewhere else.

Time crawled by. The three returned to the plane. When Idared handed one of their box lunches to her, Wilframia's face lit up.

"Thanks," she said. "I love these things."

The passengers started eating.

"I wish we could get going right now," said Wilframia between bites, "but the fuel truck still hasn't come by."

The pilot was on the radio asking about the delay as Idared told her the things they had seen and heard: the place was tense and pro-Paradise.

After another waiting period a fuel truck came along and began filling the port wing tank. Harris snorted.

"What a cushy job," he said. "There's threebs, but only the one kimmie's ottin'."

Wilframia looked out the window. Two men were loafing in the truck while one did the work.

"Must be a union thing," said Wilframia.

After the tank was full, the truck scooted over to the other side of the aircraft to fill the other one. The wolves were agitated, their tranquilizers having long since worn off. Wilframia and Idared were talking about using drugged snacks on them when there came a knock at the door.

"All done," said the pilot, moving toward the door. "I just have to sign for it." He opened the door, took the clipboard proffered by the hardworking fuel-man. Wilframia glanced out Idared's window and saw that the truck was empty. The pilot returned the clipboard to the man, who stepped away as the two other men rushed in with snubnose pistols drawn.

"Don't move!" said the first one. "We just want the wolves."

The second man's face looked familiar to Wilframia, but wildly out of context under a fuel-man's cap. His long hair had been cut to a stubble. Her heart skipped a beat and she put a name to it.

"Hello, Count Prairie dog," she said, her face drawn.

The count seemed pleased at being recognized in spite of his disguise.

"Ah, hello . . . guttersnipe."

"Let's shoot the chasers and get out," said the

first man.

"Don't shoot the plane!" cried the pilot.

"No, Stu," said the count to his henchman. He turned to the pilot and said, "We will not shoot your plane. You will help us move them out. And you." He pointed his pistol at Harris.

"Yibe, sure," said Harris. "I don't want any trouble."

"You two, sit down," said the henchman to the women.

"This is illegal," said Wilframia.

The count laughed.

"I'm not worried about that," he said. "I'll see you in court, tomorrow or next thirtnight."

It was awkward for the gunmen because the place was so small. The pilot and Harris unstrapped the first container, then the pilot took the lifting poles at the back, Harris took the ones in front, and they moved forward with a lurch.

The count was over by the cockpit, keeping a watch out the open door and following the progress inside. The wolf was scrabbling around as the carriers lurched again. The left pole handle forcefully caught the henchman in the stomach, and as he doubled over Harris fell on top of him and the container fell on Harris's legs. Idared was pulling a fire extinguisher from the bulkhead when Wilframia pulled the release pin on the container and Fenris burst out.

He was there for an instant of teeth, eyes, and fury, and then he was out the door. The count, who had shrunk back into the cockpit, rushed out the door in pursuit.

Idared clubbed Stu's head with the fire extinguisher, knocking him out. "Let's get out of here!" said Wilframia to the pilot. "Fly the plane!" She went to the door and saw Fenris running, no, he was bounding in the low gravity, each leap taking him ten meters across the airfield in the direction of the refugee tent city.

Feet planted, Count Prairie dog took aim at the wolf, but a package truck scurried from the right and skidded to a stop, blocking his view.

"Move, damn you!" he shouted, running forward to clear the vehicle. The driver was in the truck's doorway shouting "Wolf!" and heads were turning, vehicles stopping, people in Fenris's path were running away, others on the periphery seemed about to give chase.

"Help, Willie!" cried Idared, as she and Harris tried to drag the unconscious henchman to the door. Wilframia dove forward and started pawing around on the floor. Harris said, "What the—?" but then Wilframia found the pistol and was heading back to the door, which made Harris cry, "Ee tah!"

At the rear of the package truck, Prairie dog took aim.

Fenris felt a glowing heat on his hindquarters and ran faster.

Prairie dog fired, launching a homing rocket.

The heat Fenris felt surged to a flashburn that made him yelp. A puff of smoke jetted outward from his fur and the spoofed rocket missed him.

Back at the plane, the props were turning, revving up. From the cockpit the pilot was shouting. "Ready to go—Close the door!" The couple nearly had their man to the door. Wilframia moved the pistol's lever from lethal to non-lethal.

The count moved over for a clear shot, braced the pistol with his other hand, and took careful aim. Then something smacked the pavement near his feet and his left leg gave out. He was falling over, his knee was in agony, and his shot went wild. He hit the ground and rolled over to look back behind him. He saw them dumping Stu out onto the pavement. He raised his pistol to shoot at them, but then he put the rage aside as the distraction it was and rolled over to try for the wolf one more time. It was too late.

Harris yanked Wilframia into the plane, snatched the pistol and tossed it out before closing the door.

"Let's go!" shouted Idared, and the plane lifted off. "Willie, that's a serious crime, you even touching a gun—non-citizen! What were you thinking?"

"Did he kill Fenris?" asked Wilframia, starting to shake.

"I don't know," said Harris. "I didn't leek." Turning to Idared, he said, "We did all right. Dump the kimmie, so we aren't kidnapping him, and my prints are on the gun now, so there's no worries on that."

"I don't care about *me*," cried Wilframia. "I care about Fenris!" Then she collapsed into convulsive sobbing, held up by Idared. "Oh Fenris, I am so sorry!"

"There, there, applehead," said Idared. "We still have one, and that is much better than none."

6. Capricorn 12: Year's End

Life at the Woodgrow Estate assumed a normality over several thirtnights, despite the unusual circumstances. Early on the gaekwara had fled for her Argyre townhouse, saying to Wilframia, "I have met you, wolf-girl, and I hope to never see you again."

That stung Wilframia even more than when she had overheard Idared say to Harris, "Deck that! Who would guess that our fisterin' Willie was an eelstig's *mink?*" They thought of her as a fighter, an almost-gangster, and were surprised to see another side of her that looked like a rich man's mistress.

Mistress. That word was suddenly in the air, said by the staff to her face: "Yes, mistress." In a way they were acknowledging her as the chief female of the house, and they could not call her by a title she did not have, nor by any of the terms for a non-citizen, but still, the simple honorific in this context had a nasty edge to it. They knew it, she knew it, and they knew she knew it.

So be it.

She grew into the role, and by mid-Winter she was clearly Mistress of the House, taking that place in the Unmasking Day ceremony. As the Laurentia cell celebrated Unmasking Day, enacting the five-part ritual on the estate grounds, there was a special charge of meaning for their own condition as well as that of the world outside the high walls surrounding them.

Solemnly they adorned the sacred tree with all the traditional finery: ornaments representing the atmospheric carbon the tree would take away with it, the animals the breathable atmosphere would support (the usual mix of sacred animals was replaced by chasers of every kind), the life and dreams of the participants. The gaekwar took the role of the grower, through ritual re-enacting the labor of his great-great-grandparents on this land. From the forest the wolves were howling, which they had been doing so frequently that nobody noticed anymore except on such an occasion.

❋ ❋ ❋

After all the celebrations, Wilframia Terran and Gaekwar Woodgrow shared a quiet interlude together on a balcony where they sipped drinks, watching the sky fade as the sun set beyond the forest.

"It seems like the end of the world," she said.

"But it is only the end of a day," said the gaekwar softly. "Or d'yee speak of the season?"

"No my lord, I mean the Technocracy—perhaps even Martian civilization."

"I seriously doubt that," said the gaekwar. "In the larger frame, the historical perspective, it is just another day for the life of the Kasei Technocracy, or perhaps another season. Who can guess the future? If this crisis lasts less than five years, it is only a bump in the road. Even if it lasts a few decades, it is likely that a revitalized Kasei will emerge. There is a slim chance that Mars will be plunged into a fifth dark age, but should it come, it would not be so dark as the Draconiera, and might even be as mild as the Astereognosis."

"I cannot help but feel responsible," said Wilframia. "Did I loosen disaster upon the world, like Hathor laying waste to humankind until she was knee-deep in blood? Or an accidental Nirgal, releasing the great flood?"

"No, no," said the gaekwar. "If anything you are more like Utnapishtim, whose large boat rode out that same deluge and delivered all the animals to safety. You are sad, impatient that we cannot release the wolves yet."

"Originally you said they would be in there for only a few thirtnights, maybe as long as a zode."

"Did I?" said the gaekwar. "I was mistaken."

"Then we were hoping for a release by the new year," said Wilframia, "and here we are, still nothing."

"It would be foolish to release them before they are protected by law," said the gaekwar.

She said nothing.

"Yes, you are sad," said the gaekwar. "But you should be proud—you have been instrumental in the completion of the Plan! Even if your family will not be recognized immediately, full citizenship is virtually guaranteed."

She nearly scoffed, but she bit her tongue.

"Thank you for your kind words, my lord, even though I think you overestimate in order to cheer me. The chasers are only Stage 353, after all. There are 70 years to go, if further stoppages can be avoided."

"True, but all the zoos have been emptied. Pouncers and scavengers have been spotted roaming Greatvalley. There is even one report of a lion in Kasei—a seizer, Stage 360! We have lived to see this historic moment—the great circle is now complete, the great work of ages is finally done."

"So it is the end of the world," she said with a wry smile.

"It is only the end of the beginning," he insisted gently. "And the beginning of a new age."

"Forgive me, but I expected celebrations and parades, citizenship—not death and destruction," said Wilframia. "Celebrations like the Hibana wedding that Idared was watching on the gree—on the monitor. *We* should have had something like that." He shot her a quizzical look, and she added, "For completing the Stage, for all the members of the society."

"A little pomp and circumstance goes a long

way," said the gaekwar. "The marriage of two prestigious houses is an important symbol in troubled times. It is better to shift attention away from the chasers right now, and anyway citizenship is not the be-all and end-all. There are plenty of people in the Poor House with illustrious names like Canelli, Soletta, and Buryman." He paused for a sip. "As for the transition, sometimes it happens the way this one is happening. Ha'yee never wondered about the Chamber of Trees in the Great Ziggurat, how it came to be destroyed? There are many different stories about what happened four thousand years ago, but my wife's family has a tradition that I have come to favor."

Wilframia's mood darkened further. She hated it when he talked about his wife.

Oblivious or cruel, the gaekwar pressed on.

"I know that the house of Woodgrow 325 is considered 'ancient' since it was founded centuries years ago, before the Age of War, but my wife's family is Meu, an archaic word for 'moss.' So they would appear to have been on Mars since before Stage 36, if one can believe that. In any event, their tradition says that when the time came for trees to be introduced to Mars there was such a terrible dissent that war broke out. It may be difficult for us to imagine Martians becoming so passionate about plant life, but now that a similar thing has happened with the animals I suppose it is easier to see how it might have happened."

"Who were the sides?" said Wilframia,

becoming interested in spite of herself. "What were they fighting about?"

"I do not know," said the gaekwar. "There must have been at least two sides. In any event, one side was victorious, and the Chamber of Trees was defaced. The Meus say that it was done by the victors because they were going against the Plan and wanted to erase every trace."

"How horrible! Then our whole world is a lie—the Plan was undone at the beginning!"

"Perhaps," said the gaekwar. "But those early trees, whatever they were, have long since gone extinct as the atmosphere and climate changed—not a trace of them remains except as the deepest strata of charcoal in the carbonmound mines. And despite the deviation, or perhaps because of it, the other terraforming stages have all been met. It has taken longer than the ancients anticipated, but it seems that the Plan has triumphed."

* * *

That night they heard howling coming from the wrong direction, and an answering chorus of howls from the pen. They assumed that one of the wolves had finally escaped, but when they checked their pen-sensors they found all wolves accounted for. All their howling had brought an outsider.

The next day they scouted around and found a pack of six dogs led by a wolf, camped outside of the pen. The wolf appeared to be Fenris. The dogs were agitated by the nine-member wolf pack in the pen, especially when Dolph the alpha-male led the pack running in a circle. Fenris brought small kills to the pen and pushed them through the metal weave fence; the dogs stayed away from the fence.

In the days that followed the dog pack broke up and the dogs left. But Fenris stayed, feeding Laurentia snacks through the fence.

Finally the day arrived and the wolf pack was released. Six wolves stayed together as a pack, but Laurentia and two others joined Fenris to run off in a different direction.

❋ ❋ ❋

The zodes rolled on: Aquarius gave way to Southern Spring; Pisces, Aries, and Taurus gave way to Southern Summer; Gemini, Cancer, and Leo gave way to Southern Autumn; Virgo, Libra, Scorpio, and Ophiuchus came and went.

That year saw the Recovery underway, and Unmasking Day was a reunion for the former housemates. Wilframia Chaser (Stage 353) had the role of carrier in the ritual, so after the gaekwar had again completed the part of grower, she was the one to drag it along the circuit to the kiln.

The wolf watchers had seen Fenris leading a group of six wolves, most of them juvenile. Laurentia was with him.

The third year's Unmasking Day found Wilframia's young daughter as the burner. With the help and guidance of her mother she set aflame the sacred tree in the kiln. The gaekwar seemed especially frail, his age already past the fifty-six years common reckoning gave for the usual Martian lifespan.

Fenris, too, was getting old. A few cracked ribs that he had gotten from tangling with bears were just a few of the signs.

By the next Unmasking Day, Gaekwar Woodgrow had died. As the Baroness Firefox acted the part of burier, shoveling dirt onto the charcoal remains of the sacred tree, to many it seemed as if she were burying the gaekwar as well. Some livestock had been lost to chasers, so the society paid out bloodmoney to avert reprisals.

The fifth Unmasking Day was the last held by the group at the estate, which had been taken over by the government since the Woodgrow line had no heir. Once again the tree was adorned and adored, cut down and carried, burned and buried. Then, at last and as always, the joyous moment arrived when the participants took off their filter masks and breathed in the air of their homeworld as if for the first time. Gifts given, games played, feasts eaten.

Fenris's skeleton lay bleaching in the sun as they took off their masks that year, but his spirit lived on in his descendants both four legged and two.

PUBLISHING HISTORY

"Freaks Like Us, Born to Rule" first appeared in *Songs for the Elephant Man,* 2019.

"Psi Prison" first appeared online at *Perihelion,* July 2016.

BOOKS BY THIS AUTHOR

Fallout Stories

A celebration for "Fallout" with nine post-apocalyptic stories spaning a spectrum from gritty realism to the more fantastic, with robots, zombies, and the like.

*"Cuban Missile Strike" is an alternate history that might be termed "Fallout 1962."

*"Cyborg Vedohtsee and the Outlaw Slick Polla" features cyborgs, robots, and zombies.

*"The Brave Little Trash-bot at the End of the World" is an odd one.

Tarendra

"Tarendra" is a pocket epic; a star-spanning Slower Than Light voyage of alien discovery and adventure in three parts, beginning with the story "Lightspeed Messenger" (published online at "Stupefying Stories Showcase" in 2014) and moving on from there in bold new directions.

Old Flames Burn Manvi

Twelve tales of action and intrigue, including:

*A space-suited adventure in "Mad Dogs of Mercury," regarding mercs on the innermost planet when a simple job goes bad.

*A literary who-done-it with "Hardboiled Proust," tracing trouble at a living history park.

*A fairy tale in "Daughter of Plant and Woman," mixing history and her story.

*An alt-history through the lens of "Hitler's Hollywood," examining the alt-cinema that led to Nazi triumph.

And more!

The Jizmatic Trilogy +

"What if Edgar Rice Burroughs wrote Naked Lunch?"

"Under the Moons of Jizma" first appeared in the magazine "Interzone" 110 in 1996, beginning the strange mash-up tale of Edgar Rice Burroughs and William S. Burroughs upon a Martian landscape. Only now can the rest of the tale be told!

"The Jizmatic Trilogy +" (plus) is an annotated edition of "The Jizmatic Trilogy," a collection of three short stories:

*"Under the Moons of Jizma"
*"The Gods of Jizma"
*"Secret Master of Jizma."

These are adventure tales in the style of a century past (circa 1912) but with strange currents of later eras. The total length is that of a short novella.

Doomsday And Other Tours

A collection of nine stories.

*"Mad Dogs Raid Mars" shows a daring commando strike against a cyber-theocracy on the Red Planet.

*"Doomsday Tours" has a zeppelin full of tourists visiting historical sad spots across a Europe that is in the process of buckling after the withdrawal of American forces.

*"It's a Long Road to the Sky Train" is about a woman who goes on a big trip across a strange landscape. Lois Tilton called it "An entertaining,

if gruesome, read, with the imaginative characters that populate the absurdly dystopian setting, and of course Marika [the heroine]" in "Locus Online Reviews," February 2015.

These stories amount to 37,000 words of content, which is the size of a long novella, or just short of a novel (at 40,000 words).